TECHNICALLY,
MURDER

TECHNICALLY, MURDER

Robert Strong

PROSPERO

Prospero Books
46 West Street
Chichester
West Sussex
PO19 1RP

A CIP catalogue record for this book is available from the British Library.

ISBN 1 902320 02 6

Also by the Author:

A Beginner's Murder

A Flight Planned Killing

A Strange Collection of Objects

Cover design by Ian Manning

Printed in Great Britain by Antony Rowe Ltd, Chippenham, Wiltshire

A Book for Hilary

SMITH, Sir Richard, 3rd Bart. (Cr 1922). B. 3rd April, 1967. son of Arthur Smith (d.1969) and Eleanor, neé Perkins of Blagworth, Lancs. Educ. Blagworth Grammar School and Lazarus College, Oxford, B.A. 1988, M.A. 1992. Assistant Teacher, Alderman Grimshaw Comprehensive, Bridgeminster 1989-96.
M. 1997, Mary, daughter of Arthur Hitchins of Bristol.

Recreations, Criminology, Aviation. Club, Bridgeminster Conservative and Constitutional.

Address: India House, Park Rd., Bridgeminster.

Chapter One

"Dearly beloved, we are gathered together in the sight of God and in the face of this congregation to join together this man and this woman in Holy Matrimony; which is an honourable estate ..."

The words of the Marriage Service from the book of Common Prayer of 1662 had not been heard in St. Michael's Church, Bridgeminster, for many years and the Rector, the Reverend Canon Bassett, had declared privately to his Curate that it would be the last. Of course, the bridegroom was a multi-millionaire and a Baronet and that made a difference. Faced with the deplorably reactionary demand he had yielded gracefully.

"I think we have the old books somewhere, Sir Richard," he had remarked in a very pained tone. "You won't want the obey bit, I suppose, Mary?"

"Oh, yes, I think so," Richard's fiancée replied brightly. "Don't you think, Rector, that there was much less divorce when it was compulsory?"

There was no answer to that, so the worthy incumbent allowed himself as much sarcasm as a Clerk in Holy Orders may indulge in and faintly asked, "You will want `The Voice That Breathed O'er Eden,' I presume?"

The Curate, the Reverend Anthea Spofforth, a warder in Holloway Prison until her recent Ordination, was naturally deeply shocked, particularly as the Rector eventually managed to avoid taking the wedding service by pleading a prior engagement. He was to address a meeting of the Christian Euthanasia Society on that particular Saturday afternoon. He was, however, perfectly willing for the Reverend Father Randall, the semi-retired Anglo-Catholic priest who had played a part in two of Sir Richard's detective cases, to take the service, but he insisted that the Reverend Anthea should be present.

"You had better be there, my dear, in case things should get out of hand."

Exactly how the majestic language of the Prayer Book could inflame a congregation to excesses, he did not explain, but the Reverend Ms. Spofforth was extremely annoyed. As part of her 'Pastoral Outreach' she had formed a very successful girls' football team and was coaching the players herself. She had, some years previously, been a very skilled goal-keeper, having at six foot one inch and with wide shoulders, certain natural advantages.

Her Saturday afternoon was quite spoiled and it was the first match of the season.

Richard had glanced at Mary as she came to his side, followed by the Matron of Honour, her sister from Canada and two of her colleagues from the Education Department in Bridgeminster as bridesmaids. She entered the Church on the arm of her brother who was in the full uniform of a Lieutenant in the Royal Navy, with sword. At Richard's side stood Clifford Fellowes in a very correct Morning Coat. Clifford, a friend since they had suffered together as teachers at Alderman Grimshaw Comprehensive (formerly Alderman Grimshaw Grammar) and now a not very successful artist, had been happy to act as Best Man, but had found it necessary to ask the Bridegroom to pay for the hire of what he called 'the rig of the day'. Richard, in a fit of generosity had told him to get himself measured for a new suit and send in the bill. In spite of the ample fee which Richard had paid him for the large portrait in oils of the late Sir Malcolm Smith, Bart, ... painted from a number of Press photographs ... Clifford Fellowes was still, and always would be impecunious.

The picture, showing a stern Sir Malcolm ... "Big Mal" to the Aussies ... standing at a table on which a willow-pattern plate bore a large pork pie, was a reminder of how the fast-food king had made his money ... and was already hung. The few people who had been privileged to have a preview of India House ... the very elegant Georgian town residence that was to be the couple's future home - had voted the portrait a great success. As in Tudor portraits the Coat of Arms which Uncle Malcolm's father had purchased from the Herald's Office when Lloyd George had made that rather shady character a baronet, was painted in one corner.

They had already sung a hymn and Father Randall in his cultured Oxford voice was telling the congregation the causes "for which Matrimony was Ordained".

"First it was ordained for the procreation of children ..." Richard tried to see Mary's face but her veil hid it: it was a subject that the shy ex-schoolteacher had not brought himself to discuss with her. He did not know that at her "hen party" ... she was, after all a very conventional bride - her bridesmaid had warned her that her titled groom would certainly demand that she produce a male heir within a year.

"Just like Prince Charles and Diana" Emma Howick commented and it was not certain that the "poor thing" that Caroline Sparkes uttered, referred to her late Royal Highness or tomorrow's bride.

Richard, too, had had a Stag Party ... a term he thought rather vulgar ... but although the few male friends present had become very jovial, there was something about the bridegroom's manner that stopped them making that kind of joke. He looked tense! At the party Richard got to know his brother-in-law to be, who was a gunnery officer in a Destroyer just back from the Adriatic. The naval brother had remained remarkably sober: perhaps he was accustomed to drinking pink gins in the Ward room in Force nine gales. He seemed a decent sort of chap and he warmly approved of his sister's choice of husband, but the two men had little in common. He was tall, slim and handsome and in his best uniform attracted the attention of the bridesmaids and other unattached females in the church. Richard, on the other hand, looked exactly what he was; a rather shy, slightly eccentric, schoolmaster, dressed up.

"Secondly it was ordained for a remedy against sin and to avoid fornication." How splendidly earthy was the language of the old Prayer Book! Richard tried another glance at his bride but she had studied the Service in advance and was prepared! Father Randall had used the word `fornication' with some relish: the bridegroom wondered how many in the congregation now knew its meaning. For the first time he felt some satisfaction that it was a sin he had never found the opportunity to commit.

He turned his head slightly to glance at the people in the more-than half-full nave ... his Aunts from Yorkshire with an assortment of second and third cousins that they had dug up; Sam Edney, the dustman who had played Watson in his first murder case, but who, unlike the famous Doctor had one of the sharpest minds Richard had ever met. Inspector Polk was there with his rather grim wife, as was Wing Commander Tufnell of the Thelwell Flying Club and Lord and Lady Gatwick were in a pew at the back of the Church. A coach had brought a large party from the village of Foxwood, led by Mrs. Pearson, the former actress Lydia Lorraine, all eager both to see Sir Richard's bride and to discover why the mystery of the village break-ins, though obviously solved, had resulted in no arrests.[1] On the other side of the aisle were Mary's friends and relations.

"Thirdly it was ordained for the mutual society, help and comfort that one ought to have of the other ..."

Here Mary did turn her head slightly and Richard could just detect her smile behind the veil.

---

[1].See *"A Strange Collection of Objects"*.

Then came the business of the vows and the ring. Canon Bassett in the "little chat" that he insisted on having with each couple that came to his church to be married, had suggested that the Prayer Book service could be adapted to allow for an exchange of rings in the modern manner, but Richard had pointed out the symbolic meaning of the ring on the bride's finger and that progressive cleric had thought it tactless to pursue the matter further. Mary promised to obey him and Richard to endow her with all his worldly goods. It was all splendidly traditional and the somewhat agnostic Baronet felt only a slight twinge of conscience when declaring that he married his bride in the Name of Father, Son and Holy Ghost.

After that it was all plain sailing: Mary's fellow choristers had been practising a wedding anthem for some weeks and Father Randall gave a short, but rather touching address on married life. They remembered that he had been married, though he never spoke of his dead wife; that he had five children, two of them, to his deep distress, divorced.

Then it came to the signing of the register in the vestry, from which they emerged to a blast from the full organ giving Mendelssohn's Wedding March. Richard had wanted to substitute something less hackneyed from Handel, his favourite composer, but Mary was adamant: she had promised to obey, but there are limits!

The sun came out as they left the Church and the photographers got to work; not only the man contracted to make the official record but pressmen from National as well as Local papers. Then it was off to the Angel Hotel where the large hall, a noble eighteenth century room, was laid out with tables, chairs and a substantial buffet and bar. Here Richard made an interesting discovery: at a wedding no one is particularly interested in the bridegroom. Folk clustered around Mary; relations who had not met for years chatted noisily and Lieutenant Hutchins attracted much attention from the fair sex: the sword was irresistible! Richard knew that at some stage he would have to make a speech but he had that safely written out on three post cards in his breast pocket. Father Randall was circulating cheerfully and even the Reverend Ms. Spofforth was more relaxed: she had been outraged by the traditional service, but outrage can be stimulating!

The buffet food was adequate but the bridegroom felt that someone should complain to the management about the sausage rolls. Mary and her brother and sister had maintained that it was the duty of the bride's family to pay the wedding expenses; the convention was one that could not be challenged, so Richard's wrath had to remain unspoken. The canapés were not too good, either.

Clifford Fellowes as best man, managed things quite well. John Hutchins made the speech that Mary's late father would have given and Richard replied suitably, but briefly. The best man's speech contained a few of the conventional suggestive jokes. There were toasts, and Richard presented the Matron of Honour, (now his sister-in-law) and the bridesmaids, with handsome pieces of jewellery. The church service had ended at about three-forty-five and it was now past six o'clock: it was time for the newly married couple's conspiracy to be put into effect.

Family and friends had been told that the honeymoon was to be spent in the Loire Valley and that, indeed, had been the original intention. The fire at the Cloche D'Or, that pearl among French country hotels, had caused a change of plans. The members of the wedding party all believed that the honeymooners would drive off at about six-thirty to reach the night ferry for Cherbourg. Clifford had actually joked about the restrictions imposed by narrow bunks! Richard's Ford, parked in the Angel's courtyard, had been given a G.B. plate and there were suit cases in the boot ... In fact the couple had different plans. They had agreed to spend the first two nights of their married life at India House and leave on the Monday morning for a caravanning honeymoon in France. A twelve foot caravan, carefully stocked, was already parked at the rear of the house: the suit cases in the car were empty.

In the hotel courtyard and surrounded by their friends, the couple took their seats in Richard's Ford Diesel. There was much throwing of rice and confetti and words of advice were given generously. Father Randall, having been well supplied with champagne, even managed a risqué bit of information.

"Did you know, my boy, that in former times the priest always blessed the bride bed. If he overdid the Holy Water it must have been quite a damper. I suppose he spoke it in Latin then: some of these new liturgy people should try their hand at a modern version," Father Randall abominated all modern liturgies.

They left the Hotel by the road that led to the ferry port but after some two or three miles reached the roundabout where two trunk roads joined. They completed the whole circuit and turned back to Bridgeminster.

"That will have fooled them all. Now we shall have two days all to ourselves."

Mary, who had fallen silent, said nothing, but squeezed his arm, which might have had unfortunate consequences, as Richard, already with his mind on other things, had a large furniture van trying to overtake him.

The handsome wrought iron gates, newly gilded, opened smoothly and Richard closed them carefully before driving the few yards up to the Georgian porch.

"You've got to carry me over the threshold, you know." A dim light had been left burning in the entrance hall and Richard's key opened the door. There was a kiss ... a surprisingly restrained one on Mary's part ... and then he inexpertly picked his bride up and carried her into the hall.

"Turn the lights on," she said as he put her down with another kiss.

Bridgeminster Electrical Services had completely rewired the old house and Richard pressed the switch which should have lit up the period chandelier, obtained, at great expense, from a firm that specialised in electrifying early candelabra. As he pressed it, the thing lit up in a brilliant blaze of light; there was a loud "bang" from the cupboard under the stairs where the meters and switches lived, and all the lights went out.!

Mary was quite surprised at the demonstration of masterful husbandly wrath that followed.

"I shall sue him for damages, see if I don't. How can we manage without electricity until Monday? There's a torch in the car; go and get it and I'll ring Hiscocks up."

Mary, exhibiting remarkable widely obedience, went meekly to fetch the torch. When she returned Richard had calmed down.

"I'll ring him up but I won't ask him to come round to-night. Tomorrow will do: we don't want electricians tramping around this evening, do we?"

"No: we've got plenty of candles and you bought those silver candle-sticks, didn't you?"

"The Aga won't work without electricity. There's an electric pump."

"What about a hot drink?"

"We can boil a kettle in the caravan, the gas bottles are full, or, I think, there's an electric cooking ring somewhere. Perhaps the power points still work and we can plug it in."

In the dining room under Uncle Malcolm's portrait they ate a candle-lit supper. Richard had bought a selection of very expensive delicacies, including a tin of caviare with a label in Cyrillic characters.

"I've never tried it ... have you?" Mary asked.

"Just once or twice. But there's a lot of things I've never tried."

"I thought there were. You won't be disappointed with me, will you? I haven't either."

"I knew that." They understood each other perfectly.

"Do you like this caviare?"

Mary spread a spoonful of the black substance on to a biscuit and popped it into her mouth.

"I suppose I could get used to it. Is it terribly expensive?"

"It certainly is: do you know, I think I prefer Gentleman's Relish."

Richard had opened a bottle of the Sancerre that Mary usually preferred to Champagne, but she had hardly touched her glass. He, too, had drunk little: he knew that he needed the courage it might give him but hadn't he read somewhere something about it reducing the ability?

There was another of the silent intervals that were becoming more frequent. Mary leaned forward across the table and her voice sounded anxious.

"Richard, there is something we haven't talked about."

"I know, darling ... lots of things ... but ..."

"I mean, about ... babies." The girls said that you'd want ... an heir .... straightaway."

"That's silly: of course I wouldn't: one day, perhaps when we've settled down. " He paused, ... "I've bought some ... things."

"I'd love to have seen you in the chemist's shop!"

"I didn't. I got them by post."

They both laughed and relaxed a bit. There was another long silence and then Mary spoke.

"Shall we not bother for a bit. I wouldn't mind if it happened ... and I could go to the clinic when we get back ... unless ..."

The "unless" alarmed her husband but he took it bravely.

"I hoped you'd say that." This was not strictly true. Richard having never known his father, found the idea of paternity alarming.

Outside it was quiet but they had not drawn the new, heavy curtains. India House was as secluded as its previous owner, an elderly maiden lady, had desired. The wind was in the South-West and they heard the chimes of the cathedral clock strike nine in spite of the new double-glazing. They looked at each other nervously.

Mary spoke first.

"It's early, but I think I'll go up. You go and ring Mr. Hiscocks and lock the doors: don't forget the one at the back."

She picked up one of the two silver candle holders and moved to the door.

"Tell them not to come too early," were her final words as she closed the door.

Her husband sat for a few minutes sipping the last of his glass of white wine. Then, tucking the electric torch under his arm he took the three-quarter full bottle and the tin of caviar and made his way through the dark hall to the kitchen. The new cooking equipment gleamed in the torch's beam and the refrigerator light came on when the door was opened: obviously it was on a different circuit from the house lighting. There would be fresh milk for breakfast. He made his way to the small room he intended to call his study, noticing that they had put his books unsorted on the new shelves. Picking up the 'phone he dialled the home of the manager of Bridgeminster Electrical Services. In his mind he had prepared what Wing

Commander Tufnell would have called a "rocket", but all he got was an answerphone.

It is difficult to be insulting to an Answerphone but Richard did his best. He wandered round the house, checking doors and windows, ending up in the dining room they had just left. He looked up at the portrait of Uncle Malcolm and turned the beam of his torch on it. The Australian pie king looked as stern as ever but perhaps Clifford Fellowes had given his eyes just a hint of humour. Young agnostics like Richard do not pray for aid, but the bridegroom hoped that "Big Mal", wherever he was, was on his side.

Upstairs Mary entered the bedroom. She had not known that Richard had been there at 8 a.m. on the wedding morning, but she soon realised it when she saw how the exotic blooms were inexpertly arranged by the bed.

There are three bathrooms in India House, all newly fitted out, the "Master Bathroom", with an incredibly large bath, opening from the main bedroom. The guest bathroom is half way down the spacious landing and a third is attached to another bedroom at the end of the corridor. Richard would have been surprised to learn that Mary had already in her own mind, christened this last facility as part of the "nursery suite".

Richard emerged from the guest bathroom where he had earlier left dressing gown, pyjamas and toilet gear. The water had run hot: the immersion heater must have been on a different circuit, too. With a light tap on the door he edged into the bedroom.

They had bought a handsome, modern, four-poster bed. A single candle lit the room and by its light he saw his bride with her hair loose upon the pillow. There was a perfume in the air that he had not known her use previously.

"You were a long time," she said.

He slipped into the bed and she put her arms round him.

"What a nice pair of pyjamas. Where did you get them?"

"They're real silk. I got them in London."

"I like them .... Ow!"

"What's the matter?"

"There is something sharp on the collar. It's a pin: you didn't take the label off."

They laughed; and whatever happened after that they never lost the hilarity of that moment.

The sunlight streaming into the room woke Richard some time before eight. Somehow, during the night he had lost the expensive pyjamas and Mary's elaborate night dress lay across the foot of the bed. She lay with her back to him; they had experimented with the idea of sleeping in each other's arms but had agreed that it was a myth created by romantic novelists. Mary's bare shoulder reminded her husband that he had not yet seen her without clothes. He was tempted to pull back the sheet but settled for a soft kiss on her neck. She stirred, woke and turned towards him: he reached for her and wondered what her first words would be. He had read that a maiden's inhibitions can be quickly lost, but still, he was quite surprised.

"Sarah said that her husband did it three times on their first night. You did it f..."

Richard stopped her words with a kiss. Sarah's husband had not been able to leave his Ontario fruit farm to come to the wedding, but family photographs showed him to be six foot three inches tall and of massive build. It was gratifying to have outclassed him, but Richard did not want to hear more about the intimate life of the giant Polish-Canadian brother-in-law. He held Mary closer.

"Oh no you don't. I'm going to cook you a full English breakfast better than the ones you got at that hotel."

She pushed back the bed clothes and escaped.

"Oh dear, I'll have to change the sheets. What a good thing we didn't go to a Hotel!"

Richard glanced hastily at the evidence of his achievement and turned his eyes away. He had not lost his inhibitions so quickly.

"Oh dear, did I hurt you terribly? I didn't realise ..."

"Silly; it's quite normal. Sarah told me."

She giggled and disappeared in the direction of the bathroom, Richard, admiring the rear view of her unclothed body, leaned back on the pillow ready to appreciate her full-frontal re-appearance.

Nothing could persuade Mary that a man did not need an immense breakfast after such a night and in fact they both made a substantial meal. The expensive coffee machine, brought from Richard's flat that had never responded to his management, worked perfectly with a woman's touch. It was all very domesticated.

* * * * *

Richard had rather hoped that Mary would spend the day dressed in flimsy garments and the flowered house-coat that suited her so well. She made it clear after breakfast that it would not do and appeared in a rather severe summer dress. Mr. Hiscocks was to arrive at eleven and that worthy, truly repentant, appeared on time with two of his men and rectified the electrical fault. They spent the rest of the morning stocking the new caravan and, carefully following the instructions in the hand-book hitched it up to the car. Lunch was a light meal, and after it, without a word of agreement, they found themselves back in the bedroom. It was when they emerged at about

4 p.m. that they found the need to fill in time! Perhaps, later in the honeymoon there might be scope for a little reading ... Richard had packed a couple of dozen paperbacks for the caravan holiday ... but surely, not on the second day? Television was obviously out of the question. He filled in an hour arranging his books on his study shelves and Mary got out a new cookery book to plan the evening meal.

The dinner was a great success. The new bride produced a homemade soup of a quality never experienced by her husband in seven years of bachelor tin opening, and the steaks from the freezer were tender.

Sitting at the candle-lit table Richard looked up at the portrait of Uncle Malcolm with a more confident stare.

After dinner they sat side by side in the deep settee in what they had so far referred to as the "other room". The splendid proportions of Georgian India House made it impossible to call it the lounge: the sitting room sounded too cottagey and "the drawing room" too grand. Perhaps it would have to remain the "other room" throughout their married life. They had switched on an electric fire as there was a touch of Autumn in the air and Richard's old record player gave out soft and romantic music. He had refused to exchange it for one that played the new disc things for he had a large collection of tapes and records. He forced himself to recognise that the urgency of the night before had passed but he knew he would soon feel amorous again. There was, after all, time to finish the coffee and the glass of Izarra that Mary was also sampling.

This contented mood was disturbed by the sound of a bell. The front door of the old house had its original heavy brass knob connected by a wire to a high-pitched bell in the entrance hall. The builders had assumed that they would want to replace it with an electric circuit, but they had both liked the old bell.

"Oh dear," Mary exclaimed, "who can it be? Nobody knows we are here."

Her husband rose and crossing the hall opened the door to the first visitor of their married life. The automatic light in the porch revealed a man of about fifty-five years, shortish, with greying hair and dressed in a rather baggy tweed suit.

His accent, although not exactly refined, was precise and had a Northern burr: Yorkshire, perhaps or Lancashire? He shifted his weight from one foot to another in a nervous manner.

"Sir Richard Smith?" he asked.

"Yes, do come in: I'm afraid I don't know your name."

"We have met, actually, though briefly. My name is Floodgate ... Dr. Floodgate. I'm the ..."

"Of course, you're the Principal of the Technical College."

The visitor winced. "We call it the College of Advanced Education now. I presented the prizes at your school's speech day when you were a teacher." Richard remembered that the College had had a number of names. Originally Bridgeminster Technical School it first became the College of Technology and Art, then the College of Further Education and just failed to become a Polytechnic. It was still universally referred to as "the Tech".

"I remember; do come in and have something. We're here in the ... well we can't decide what to call it; perhaps "parlour" would do. My wife, Mary. Darling this is Doctor Floodgate from the College ... he's our first visitor."

"Lady Smith: I'm very sorry to disturb you both. I heard that you were going away soon and I had to call on your husband. You see, I have something rather important to consult him about."

It was, except in ribald remarks at the wedding reception, the first time that Mary had been addressed by her title and she blushed prettily. Richard rescued her.

"Do sit down, Dr. Floodgate. This is a liqueur I brought back from France: there's Green and Yellow and I can't decide which I like best! There's coffee if you prefer ... it's still hot."

"Just coffee, please: with milk and sugar."

Mary poured the visitor a cup and he sat back in the easy chair and sipped.

" May I ask you how you knew we were here? "Officially we were to be on last night's boat for Cherbourg, but we changed our plans a bit - keeping it secret, or so we thought."

"Inspector Polk told me."

"I'll have a word with Jim Polk.

Of course we are delighted to see you," he added hastily, "but ..."

"He wasn't exactly breaking a secret. He told me I ought to see you."

"I don't understand."

"May I tell you the whole story ... in strict confidence."

Floodgate hesitated for a moment and then went on speaking rapidly.

"It can hardly be criminal, I suppose ... but it is a very strange business. I did not think it serious until I got the letter and then I thought it better to go to the Police and Inspector Polk suggested that I should come and see you. If it hadn't been Mr. Fordham I wouldn't have been so disturbed ... a Head of Department, you know!"

This made little sense; the man was obviously troubled.

"Perhaps you could begin at the beginning?"

The visitor put down his coffee cup and seemed to pull himself together.

"I'm sorry: nothing like this has happened to me before. The Inspector said that there was no evidence of anything criminal in spite of the letter, but he said you would be sure to be interested."

"Very kind of him."

"I've never had anything like this happen in the past. I've been Principal for fourteen years and the College has grown so much that it's not easy to get to know all the members of the Staff ... three hundred full-time lecturers, you know."

Dr. Floodgate, Richard knew, was a heroic empire builder, but not particularly popular with his Staff and also that he had a reputation for being somewhat ruthless in disciplinary matters ... at least as far as current employment legislation permitted him. Bridgeminster had enjoyed reading newspaper reports of the Tribunal Decision, re-instating a young lecturer in Sociology who had been dismissed for making a seventeen year old student pregnant. The good Doctor was naturally not so hard on his students: they were too valuable.

"How did your problem begin?" Richard asked.

"You must excuse my confusion. We don't normally have a lot of troubles at the College: drugs, of course from time to time and one or two cases of theft or fraud."

"But this is different?"

"I will start at the beginning. This is the second week of term. Last Monday morning I got a letter from Edward Fordham saying that he would not be returning. Just three lines; that was all!"

"He was the Head of Department that you mentioned."

"Business Studies and Computer Science. One of the best qualified men in the College. He has first-class honours degrees in Economics and Law and had a very important Job in a merchant bank before he joined us. Frankly, I was surprised that a man in his position wanted to come into Further Education, but I suppose at fifty the high pressure life begins to pall. It's a Scale Seven Department but he must have taken a considerable drop in salary. There were three hundred applicants for the post."

"And he has just disappeared? Was he a married man?"

"Yes; no children: his wife never came to College functions."

"His wife has gone?"

"Yes; I went round to his house that evening and it was shut up. I tried again on the Wednesday and there was a house agent's board up ... For Sale."

"Which Agent?"

"Cringles."

"Did you go to see them?"

"Yes, but Mr. Cringle would give me no information. He had his instructions, he said."

Richard considered for a moment. "But surely, Dr. Floodgate, teachers have nervous breakdowns. I can remember feeling pretty low after sessions with 4 D on a Friday afternoon. You must have had one crack up in the past."

"Occasionally, yes, but Fordham didn't do any teaching. None of the Heads of Departments do and the Principal Lecturers do very little ... all this administration, you know!"

Richard reflected that the Public might be surprised to know that so many well qualified ... and well paid, teachers, spent most of their time doing work that could be performed by reasonably able clerks.

"You said there was a letter?"

"That was what made me worried. Until it came I was merely very annoyed; I was going to be so embarrassed when I reported to the Governors."

"The letter?"

Floodgate took an envelope from his pocket. It was a cheap, brown one of the sort tradesmen use to send in their bills. The message was written on a piece of unlined paper that might have been torn out of a note-book.

The writer had used a ball point and the message was:-

YOU'RE BETTER OFF WITHOUT
HIM HE WAS UP TO NO GOOD

"HE, I suppose must be Mr. Fordham," Richard observed. "It could be a mischievous student ... or even a disgruntled member of staff. When did you say you got the letter?"

"On the Wednesday morning."

"That was the twelfth. The letter is post-marked the ninth and it is a second class stamp. The sender must have posted it before you knew the man was missing."

"I didn't think of that."

"When did you go to the Police?"

"I rang Inspector Polk at his home last night. I had been worrying about it since I got the letter and my wife advised me to. He'd just got back from your wedding reception ... and he said it was just the sort of case you'd ..."

"I bet he said `like to play about with'."

Dr. Floodgate smiled for the first time ... a rather strained smile, and Richard went on.

"The Police don't really approve of amateurs, you know."

"Oh, I think he was quite impressed by your work. He said that you had been of great help in several cases."

"You say you spoke to him last night. How on earth did he know that we had come here?"

"He said to remind you that the Police have eyes everywhere. I think he saw your car coming back into the city after he left the reception."

"Yes, I see." Richard swallowed the last drop of his liqueur and put down his glass.

"Dr. Floodgate, it seems to me that you have not got any evidence of anything criminal going on at the College or even any improper activity. It is surprising that a senior member of our staff should leave without proper notice but it just might be something simple to explain: teachers are pretty temperamental, aren't they? We are off tomorrow morning but when I ... we ... get back in about three weeks time ..."

"You will look into it?"

"You must find some excuse for me to hang about the College. Perhaps I ought to join one of your do-it-yourself classes. All our lights fused last night, you know."

"Why not teach a class? You taught English Lit., I believe and our General Studies Department could fix you up with one. We pay £14 an hour."

"It will help with the house-keeping. What about Mary?"

"I could join a cookery class. My mother used to say you have to feed the brute."

"Good idea: give me your private telephone number Dr. Floodgate and I'll give you a ring occasionally while we're away to learn if there are any developments. I shouldn't worry too much about it ... it could be something quite innocent. May I keep that letter?"

"Thank you, Sir Richard." The man rose to go, uttering conventional good wishes for their marriage. Richard saw him out, returning thoughtfully to join Mary on the sofa.

"Well, that will take your mind off other things, won't it?"

"Oh no, it won't:" he moved closer.

"No, not here. I'm going to have a bath. There's only that poky little shower in the caravan so it will be the last one for a bit."

"I'll come and join you presently."

"Oh, that's why you had that huge bath put in. I thought so at the time. Don't forget the tickets and the passports for the morning."

Richard, marvelling at the way in which an excessively virginal fiancée can rapidly develop, sat for some twenty minutes considering the story Floodgate had told him. It did not seem the moment to worry about it too much and, locking the doors he went upstairs.

The king-size bath was entirely satisfactory!

Chapter 2

Richard had tried a few practice runs with the caravan
hitched up but it was a nervous driver who edged the
'outfit', (as experienced caravanners call their equipment)
up the ramp and on to the car deck. He had booked a
cabin in case an autumnal gale should blow up but the
day was fine and clear and the French coast came in sight
soon after the Needles disappeared astern. They walked
the deck, lunched at the 'Captain's Table' Restaurant and
played baccarat in the small casino set up on 'C' deck.
Richard ended £3.75 down and decided that he did not
like losing money. Mary won! They spent the first three
days of their honeymoon at the camp site at St. Vaast le
Hogue, some twenty miles east of Cherbourg. The French
consider September to be an out-of-season month and
there were few other occupants of the camp, and those
mainly elderly English couples enjoying Autumn
holidays. The restaurants were good and the van's cooking
arrangements were seldom used. With no other caravan
within thirty feet or so, their lovemaking became quite
uninhibited until a young German couple in a battered
motor-caravan parked about twenty feet away and they
realised how inadequately sound-proofed are caravans.
They remembered with pleasure the thick walls of India
House.

On the fourth day they left Normandy for the Loire
Valley and found a riverside camp only a few miles from
the Cloche d'Or where they were welcomed with Gallic
enthusiasm by M. and Madame Lebel and M. Biron,
Madame's aged father. The fire damage had almost been
made good: the famous restaurant had re-opened and the
Patron promised that they could be put up in the Hotel
for the last few days of their honeymoon. It was impossible
to get Lebel to understand that the wife of a Baronet was

not usually addressed as "Milady": he had rather taken to Richard's bride and even invited her to inspect his kitchen, allowing her to take copies of several of his recipes.

They found to their surprise that the last week of their stay passed more slowly. They spent rather more time reading the paperbacks or the French newspapers and twice they went to a cinema. Richard spent some hours sitting in a deck-chair ... the weather was still pleasantly warm ... thinking about the visit of Dr. Floodgate. Twice he telephoned the Principal at his home, but nothing further had occurred to disturb the peace of the College. On the second Monday in October they caught the morning boat at Cherbourg.

There were no English papers on the ferry and it was not until they drove through Bridgeminster that a billboard caught Richard's eye.

COLLEGE DEATH MYSTERY, it announced.

You cannot stop at a corner shop when towing a caravan, but as soon as it was safely parked Richard dashed out to get an evening paper and that edition carried the story.

The dead man was one Henry Seaforth, Head Caretaker, (or rather Senior Maintenance Officer,) of the College. He had been found dead in the entrance hall of the Administrative Building by one of the caretaking staff whose duty it was to arrive at seven a.m. and unlock doors. He had been shot through the heart at close range, the heavy calibre bullet passing through his body and breaking a window pane. Police inquiries were continuing.

The couple sat at their kitchen table eating a 'high tea' of poached eggs on toast. The rich meals served at the

Cloche d'Or and other French restaurants had at least temporarily, made them feel less inclined to eat a large evening meal. Mary had declared that she was afraid to face her bathroom scales but her husband countered by suggesting gallantly that a little extra roundness added to her charms.

"Do you suppose the murder has something to do with Dr. Floodgates problem," Mary asked?

"I don't know. I was thinking of going round to the College tomorrow to see about those classes he wants me to take."

"And I could enrol for cookery. I want to try some of those recipes that M. Lebel gave me. They say that the Senior Lecturer in cookery was once a chef at the Ritz."

"I'm already utterly satisfied with married life but if you are going to do Cordon Bleu meals, I shall be out of this world."

"Literally, if you get over-weight. Perhaps I ought to enrol for `Cookery for Weightwatchers'. Later that evening the door bell rang: it was Inspector Polk."

Chapter 3

Inspector Polk sat in the corner of the deep settee and reflected that matrimony certainly altered a man's life. When he had in the past called on the bachelor baronet he had been given just as much whisky in his glass, but the glass had not always been quite clean and certainly not polished. The new wife had personally seen to providing him with an extra cushion for his back and a plate of savoury biscuits lay beside his drink. The room was warm, too, for Mrs. Barlow, the daily help that they had engaged, had switched on the central heating before their arrival. Polk's own wife was not one to overdo the home comforts and he appreciated the attention.

"How did you know we were back?"

"You keep asking me questions like that. I've told you ..."

"Yes, I know, `eyes everywhere'; but ..."

"If you don't want people to see your caravan parked outside you'd better put corrugated iron on those pretty gates. I was driving past."

"Well it's nice to see you ..."

"And you: and the new Lady Smith."

"Do call me Mary, Jim."

"Here's health and good luck to both of you. Now ..."
Polk took out a notebook.

"I suppose you can guess why I called."

He had drained his glass and Richard hastened to refill it.

"I told Floodgate to put you on to his little problem 'cos I thought it was in your line. Not criminal, naturally, but full of human interest, as they say. That doesn't mean we want you poking your nose into the murder business, but if you're going to be hanging about the College you might pick up something. But I suppose you're bound to take an interest," he added gloomily.

"Don't you think the two things are connected," Mary asked?

"Don't see why they should be. This shooting looks more like a regular contract killing ... very neat job. Don't tell me that a lot of neurotic teachers would be involved in it."

"Why should a contract killer shoot a caretaker?"

"Well we don't know what the murderer was after. There's a lot of valuable stuff in that College: computers, for instance. Enquiries have only just begun; we made them close the College for today which upset a lot of people; the organiser of the Beginners' Bridge class was really abusive!"

"I've signed up to take classes at the College: Tuesday and Wednesday afternoons, I think."

"Leaving the new wife on her own?"

"I'm going to cookery classes,' Mary put in. "Wednesday and Thursday."

"Well, let me know it you pick up anything. I don't know how you make these lucky guesses, but they helped us quite a bit in that Park case ... and, (here Polk paused) and in that aerodrome affair. There's a story going round that you cleared up that funny business at Foxwood: `No Comment', I suppose?"

"By the way, what time was the man killed?"

"Around midnight, the Doctor says. Died instantly; big calibre bullet."

Polk remained a little longer ... he had not yet had his usual third whisky, but he had nothing further to tell them.

The next day was Tuesday and Richard, with a sheaf of notes in the battered briefcase that he thought he had discarded for ever when he left Alderman Grimshaw Comprehensive, reported to the Head of the General Studies Department at 1.45 p.m. He was taken to a bleak classroom with large white board of the sort that requires a special crayon; they had given him one but it would not work. The class was supposed to begin at 2 pm. but the students drifted in by stages and by 2.15 was complete. There was a register to be marked and Richard discovered that the members were studying for A Levels in various science subjects, it having been decided that an exposure to 'Liberal Studies' was necessary if they were to impress University Selection Boards. They obviously deeply resented the programme! He told them that he intended to give them an outline of English Literature from the earliest times and began with Beowulf ... having that morning obtained photo-copies of some pages of that work to give to each student. They endured Beowulf with fortitude but their teacher soon discovered that not one of them had the slightest knowledge of English History nor indeed that of any other nation. Not one knew whether the Saxons or the Romans came first ... "gave up History in the third year" was the usual excuse ... although one claimed to have done a Module on Transport through the Ages and got a Grade C. An attempt to get a discussion going was a complete failure and promising to introduce them to Chaucer in Thursday's class, he dismissed them and made his way to the staff-room.

The College staff room is large and comfortable with a pleasant view across the sports field to the Cathedral. It, is, however, not much used by the lecturers, most preferring to take their breaks in the corners of laboratories, store cupboards and other convenient hiding places. Previous Principals had tried to eradicate the custom, very reasonably believing that when their subordinates were out of sight they were probably conspiring against authority, but it had not been possible to suppress the practice.

A dozen or so were drinking tea and one was Howard Emerson. Howard's help had been vital in the solution of the Thelwell Airfield case, his unauthorised loan of a College Geiger Counter leading to a vital piece of evidence. Richard sank into an easy chair next to the Senior Lecturer in Chemistry.

"Richard! Back at the chalk-face!"

"It's not chalk now: funny crayons that don't work."

"I know, not half as good as chalk and they cost the earth. You wouldn't stand in the way of Progress, would you? I heard you were going to teach a class but I suppose there's an ulterior motive ... poor Harry Seaforth's murder, I presume."

"No, not at all." Richard considered. "Look, Howard, you're a discreet sort of fellow and you'll keep quiet about it. The Principal asked me to look into this business of a staff member just ... well, absconding is the word, I think."

"Very odd: there's been a lot of talk. Still it's not exactly criminal, is it? I often wish I could bunk off!"

"Did you know the man?"

"I didn't know him very well; from what I've heard I don't think anyone did. I believe he was something quite big in the City at one time; something to do with foreign exchange, they said. He was terribly well qualified and I suppose he wanted a quiet life. Very odd, I must say."

They finished their tea and left the staff-room; Howard to teach another class and Richard, his day's work over to make his way home. How, he wondered, had he been able to teach six lessons a day in former times?

Richard left the College as the students began to pour out. Most were local youngsters but there were students from Africa, India, the Middle East and Japan. Before leaving he had obtained the address of the former Head of Department from the College Office and drove home making a detour for a quick look at the small, detached house on the Larkhill estate that had been the home of

Edward Fordham. Outside a board announced that it was for sale and that Cringles were sole agents.

At breakfast next morning ... Mary had insisted that they both should try to lose some weight and served only coffee, toast and marmalade ... Richard put to her the problem that had been occupying his mind.

"I must try to see the inside of Fordham's house: can you think of an excuse?"

"Well it's up for sale: ask the agent."

"He'll know I've just bought this place: all these agents have a grapevine."

"Tell him you want to buy a place for one of your aunties: he'll know you've got lots of money."

"It might work but he's sure to know I'm interested in crime."

"Ask to see several houses; then he won't be suspicious."

"Will you come with me?"

"You've forgotten: I've got my cookery class this morning. I bought a new apron yesterday."

At 9 a.m. Mary went off on her motor-scooter ... India House has garaging for three cars in the old coach house but Mary had not yet found time to learn to drive a four-wheeled vehicle ... and Richard made his way to the office of Cringle's Estate Agency. It was a small affair and in the days when banks and building societies were making frenzied bids for the larger concerns, it had attracted no offers. Mr. Cringle, the third of that name to run the firm, was something of a local character. He was sixtyish, small, thin and lugubrious, with the scarlet nose of the serious drinker. He had been heard to say that if he could sell a hundred houses in a year he was content and indeed he probably seldom exceeded that figure. His only member of staff was a bony female of uncertain age who was generally supposed to be his mistress, Mrs. Cringle having long departed this life. His office consisted of two rooms in a converted cottage in Priory Street.

If the Estate Agent suspected Richard's motives he showed no signs of it: indeed the red nose seemed to twitch at the prospect of a sale.

"A suitable home for an elderly lady ... living alone, I presume? We have a very nice modern terrace house near the City centre."

"I think my Aunt would prefer a detached house; but one without a large garden. She has a touch of Arthritis, you know."

Richard had noticed that the Fordham house had only a small plot attached. He also made a mental note to remember the ailments he had given to the fictitious Aunt.

"Now this," Mr. Cringle enthused, "is a most desirable residence. On the inner ring road and very handy for the shops."

"My Aunt keeps cats. There would be traffic."

"Ah: well what about this house? Just on the market and the vendor looking for a quick sale. On the Larkhill estate; quiet and very much in demand. We have sold a number of them recently."

Mr. Cringle had actually sold one.

Richard studied the printed sheet with its photograph of the house of the missing Fordham.

"Yes, that looks interesting. May I see it?"

"No problem: the vendor has had to go away suddenly and has given us the sole agency. I have the keys: would you like to see it this morning?"

Mr. Cringle led the way to his car park and within a few minutes they arrived at the former home of the missing Head of Department. The agent's key admitted them to the entrance hall where a number of letters lay on the door-mat. Cringle picked them up and put them into the small brief case he carried. Most seemed to be circulars but Richard noticed that one carried a foreign stamp, bright yellow in colour: he could not identify its origin.

The house was fully furnished, pictures on the walls, beds made up and books on shelves.

"Will the vendors be removing their furniture?" Richard asked. "My Aunt has been living in a small flat and would probably be willing to buy some of it."

"They have gone abroad," Mr. Cringle replied. "I believe they have no intention of returning to England: it is a rather unusual situation."

"There seem to be quite a few personal possessions remaining." Richard observed, as he opened a built-in wardrobe in what the agent described as the `master bedroom', where several suits of clothes still hung neatly.

"That will be no problem," Cringle replied. "I have the sole agency and authority to sell."

"Would it be possible to have a word with the owners? You say they have gone abroad: their telephone number, perhaps. I think my Aunt would like to know about ... well, the neighbours and things like that."

"I'm afraid I can't do that. I have my instructions, you see."

Mr. Cringle had in his early days lost several commissions by allowing purchasers to communicate with vendors.

The Estate Agent had begun the tour of inspection by taking his client to the first floor: next they descended the stairs and the kitchen equipment was demonstrated. Howard Emerson had said that Fordham had been a high earning Executive in a merchant bank before descending to Further Education but the house and its fittings did not seem particularly luxurious. The lounge was comfortable but not pristine: indeed some of the furniture was slightly shabby. There were bookshelves against one wall: Mr. Fordham had obviously been a golfer as there was a shelf full of works by, or about, famous professionals and no less than two sections of travel books, mainly on Africa.

The house seemed not to reflect the personality of the owners: "anonymous" was the word that came to Richard's mind.

It was necessary to keep up the pretence that there was an Aunt in the background that might buy.

"£120,000 was the asking price, I believe."

"Well, yes, Sir Richard, but I have reason to believe that the vendors would like a quick sale ... a near offer might well be acceptable: a very near offer, I mean."

"Quite so, Mr. Cringle. Perhaps I ought to see the garage and the garden: my Aunt still drives, you know."

There was nothing to be learned from either.

That evening they ate the meal that Mary had prepared in the cookery class. It was a Hungarian Goulash, that heated up nicely in the microwave.

"What did you find in the Fordham house?" Mary asked.

"Not much. Just an ordinary house on the Larkhill estate. Not very luxurious."

"Did the man say where they had gone?"

"Overseas, somewhere; he was very reticent."

Next day they both were to go to the College. Richard's class was again at 2 p.m. and Mary's cooking at 2.30. The College Catering Department has a training restaurant where young people practise the art of waiting at table. After breakfast Richard rang and booked a table for 12:30.

The 'Ascot Room' at the College has twenty tables and a small bar; the 'Epsom' is merely a Cafeteria. The food is generally excellent value at £6.50 for a three course lunch but the service can be erratic. The young waiters are taught the correct ritual with fork and spoon when serving hot dishes and the luncher is apt to watch apprehensively as the youth struggles to place the viands on his plate, which, naturally, makes the lad even more nervous. When it is a ladle of very hot soup the situation can become tense.

They had got to the 'sweets from the trolley' stage and Mary was recommending (in the interests of weight-watching) the fresh fruit salad rather than the cream-ridden gateau, when Dr. Floodgate entered the restaurant and spotting Richard and Mary approached their table. He looked anxious.

"I was hoping to get in touch with you today. You have your class at two. Could you come to see me after it?"

The Principal made some polite remarks and retired to the further end of the room, where a table had been set apart for him and his guests ... obviously a group of bureaucrats from the Ministry of Education or some important quango; the entertaining of an endless succession of officials occupying a significant proportion of Dr. Floodgate's time. He had as a result something of a weight problem!

Richard and Mary went back to watching the student waiter doing dangerous things with the coffee pot.

The students came no earlier to the English Literature class but neither were they later. They were in their second year and knew exactly what they could get away with. Richard began with Chaucer's Miller's Tale, reading both from a modern translation and the poet's own words. Most thought it rather cute, but the girls in the class thought the marriage of the sprightly Alison and the elderly carpenter, disgusting. At 3 p.m., promising to introduce them to the Wife of Bath next week, he dismissed them and made his way to the Administration Wing and the Principal's study.

"You have heard about the murder: do you think it is connected with Fordham's disappearance?" were Dr. Floodgate's first words.

"I don't see why it should. In any case that is a matter for the Police."

"You helped the Police in the Abbey Gardens case."

"Yes, but that was an accidental involvement, more or less."

"Does anything occur to you?"

"Not really: I visited Fordham's, house: it's up for sale as you know. I pretended that I was looking for a place for an aged Aunt. There was nothing of interest ... except ..."

" Except?"

"Well, ... no nothing of importance, really ..." Richard paused ... "Tell me Dr. Floodgate, I should think that you have in the College experts in very many different fields."

"Pretty well: we've got builders, engineers, accountants, a lawyer or two ... not very successful ones: they wouldn't work for our salary scale. All the usual science subjects, naturally ... I did bio-chemistry ... and we have art, music and drama departments. You have just seen our catering section at work: did you have a good lunch, by the way?"

"Excellent, thankyou. Do you have an expert in philately?"

The Principal looked puzzled. "Stamp collecting: why?"

"Just curiosity."

"There's Mr. Tredwin: he teaches Economic History in the General Studies Department. He ran an evening class in Philately for several years but I think interest in the subject must have declined. He couldn't raise the statutory twelve last year."

"Twelve?"

"You must have twelve students before the class can be authorised ... not economic, otherwise."

"I've only ten in my class."

"That's a full-time class: different rule."

"I see. What sort of a man was Henry Seaforth?"

"I thought you said there was no connection between his death and your problem."

"There almost certainly isn't but perhaps ..."

"Harry Seaforth has been at the College for a good many years: he was here when I came. He was promoted to Head Caretaker when old Charlie Meadows retired. He is ... was ... very efficient and managed his staff well. The cleaners are mostly part-time."

"Where did he live?"

"There's a bungalow in the College grounds ... behind the new gymnasium. We shall have to ask his widow to move out eventually but I think we can get the Council Housing Department to find her a flat."

The Principal had glanced at the clock on the wall and Richard thought it time to leave.

"One last question: you have lost a Head of Department ... could you have had any students disappearing recently?"

"That happens all the time. They drop out for all sorts of reasons; often just before their exams. We had a Chinese boy once, name of Wong, if I remember rightly. He was so brilliant that he frightened his lecturers and then got lovesick and went off to join his girlfriend somewhere."

"Any this term?"

"I wouldn't have the figures. Miss Penfold, the Assistant Registrar will have all the details: ask her."

Floodgate seemed to remember something.

"I have of course told the Administrative Staff to let you have any information you require."

"So I could see the personal records of all the members?"

"Yes ... er ... you will be discreet, I'm sure."

"Including your own?"

"Really, Sir Richard, I find that intolerable! It was I who asked you to investigate."

The Principal had stood up and Richard also rose.

"There must be complete confidence, Dr. Floodgate: otherwise I must ask you to let me drop the investigation."

The man was angry. Richard well knew that since Dr. Arnold imposed his will on Rugby School, Headmasters and Principals had found it hard to cope with any form of opposition, and the silent struggle lasted for some moments.

"Very well, Sir Richard: all information. I will tell Miss Penfold."

The General Studies Department, which was responsible for Richard's literature class had the untidiest staff-room the visitor had ever seen. Desks were piled high with scripts ready for marking and there were forms and charts, the completion of which occupied a large part of the teacher's time. A poster pinned to the door urged all lecturers to take part in a giant 'demo' of workers and teachers against the Education Cuts. Mr. Tredwin was seated at a table gazing gloomily at a large sheet of paper on which a time-table of classes had been traced.

"Mr. Tredwin: my name is Smith ... a part-time teacher ... in this department, actually."

Tredwin was in his late fifties. He was extraordinarily thin and there was also a sort of hungry look about his features. Later Richard was to learn that he was a product of the London School of Economics of the Fifties and an unreconstructed Marxist. He looked up.

"Ah, yes: the plutocratic, noble sleuth; called in by the Yorkshire Ripper."

What might have been a startling opening was said with a friendly smile.

"The Ripper," Richard stammered.

"Floodgate: he comes from Huddersfield. That's what we call him mostly in this department. There are other names though! That's the kindest."

"You know why I am here then, Mr. Tredwin?"

"I can guess: Harry Seaforth: by the way the name's Len; you're Dick, I think."

"Richard, usually. No, it's not the murder; the Principal asked me to try to find out why the Head of the Business Department left suddenly."

"Fordham; another lackey of the capitalist oppressors. He was once a sort of fat cat in the City. God knows why he came down here to a teaching job; they tell me that he made a fortune in some bank and didn't need to work: masochism, I suppose!"

"His home didn't seem very luxurious."

"He lived on that Larkhill estate, didn't he? All lace curtains, patios with barbecues and Ford Sierras. How beastly the Bourgeois is."

The only reply that Richard could think of was, "Quite."

The unreformed Stalinist went on.

"Why did you come to ask me about Fordham? I know more about poor Harry Seaforth; a genuine worker."

"I didn't come to ask you about him either. I heard you were a keen stamp collector and I wanted to know ..."

"You must be joking. Or are you a philatelist?"

"Let me explain: I saw a letter with a bright yellow foreign postage stamp: could you suggest a possible origin?"

"You mean a letter posted at the present time?"

"Yes, a letter not a package."

Tredwin's manner had quite changed. The cynical tone was gone and he showed himself the true enthusiast.

"I specialize in early British Colonial issues. Perhaps you would like to see my collection: I started it when I was twelve. I'm chairman of the Bridgeminster Philatelic Society."

"But the yellow stamp ..."

"I wouldn't know but I can easily look it up. I've got all the usual catalogues. These new republics in Asia and Africa often issue very gaudy stamps. A very bright yellow, you say?"

"Yes, and rather larger than an English stamp."

"Give me a ring this evening ... no ... come round for a drink and I'll look it up."

He scribbled an address on a memo-pad and handed the paper to Richard.

"I don't know what my wife will say when I bring a member of the aristocracy home. She's rather more extreme than I am."

"I'm of impeccably lower-middle-class origins. My grandfather bribed Lloyd George to make him a Baronet and my uncle made a fortune selling cheap meat pies and Hamburgers to the Australians."

"Well, don't worry, Dick: we'll tolerate you until the revolution and then liquidate your class ... fairly painlessly."

Mr. Tredwin strongly approved of the Soviet extermination of the Kulaks, but was actually the most kind-hearted of men.

"We'll expect you then this evening any time will do; we don't have dinner at eight like the toffs do."

* * * * *

Miss Penfold, the Assistant Registrar did not approve of Sir Richard Smith, nor of granting him access to her records. She was about forty and might have been attractive if her manner had not been designed to intimidate all comers.

"What do you want to know, Sir Richard?"

Richard would like to have said, "Oh do call me Richard," or even "Dick".

Few people were on Christian name terms with Miss Penfold: hardly anyone knew that her's was an unlikely 'Maralyn'.

"I would like to know, Miss Penfold, the names of any students who failed to return to the College at the beginning of this term ... particularly overseas students. I believe there are a number from several foreign countries."

"One hundred and eighty-seven: seventeen failed to continue with their courses. I have to notify their Embassies: I made out this list today."

From a folder on her desk she took a paper and handed it to Richard.

"You will see that there is one from Hong Kong, two from Singapore and the rest from various African States. It is, of course, possible that some of them will return in the next week or so. I will go and get a photo-copy of this list."

She left the room for a few moments and returned with the copy. Richard took it and asked for the file on Edward Fordham which she reluctantly handed over. As he took his leave he got the impression that she was about to say something, but in the end no word was uttered.

There is a short story by the inimitable Saki called simply "Tea". A young bachelor proposes marriage to a Bohemian-type girl after drinking tea from earthenware mugs in her somewhat squalid studio. How refreshingly different she seemed from the elegant maidens that his Mother had encouraged him to call upon, who served it in porcelain cups and with elaborate ritual. Alas, after the honeymoon he found that his bride had changed her ways!

Mary had never lived a Bohemian life but her flat had been comfortable rather than elegant and she had certainly often poured tea into thick beakers. Now, like the Edwardian bride she sat behind a silver tea-pot and the Royal Doulton tea service that had been her brother's wedding present.

"How did the cookery class go?" Richard asked.

"We did sponge cake. Mine was rather flat: ... look."

It *was* flat but her husband gallantly took a slice.

"Did you hear anything interesting?"

"They were talking about the murder. Mr. Blenkinsopp said that he knew the man who was killed."

"Is Blenkinsopp the cookery lecturer?"

"No, he's in the class: the only man. He's a bachelor and the other women do make jokes about him."

"Poor man!"

"No, I think he likes it. He's a retired teacher with ever so many degrees and diplomas. They say he never had time to find a wife with all that studying. He's Doctor Blenkinsopp, too."

"What did he say about Seaforth?"

"Not very much, really: he did say that he was once a Police Officer and had to leave the Force because he was injured when trying to arrest same robbers."

"Which Police Force?"

"He didn't say."

Richard gave Mary a short account of his day's detecting.

"I talked to a man at the College who's keen on stamp collecting. I wanted to know about that letter from some foreign country I told you about; the one on the mat in Fordham's house."

"Did he know?"

"He's going to look up his catalogues. He's asked me round to his place this evening. He didn't suggest that I bring you along but I don't suppose he'll mind. He's very Left Wing.

"So was my Dad. He was a Labour Councillor when we lived at Garthwaite. Mum was Conservative: she wouldn't have minded me marrying a Baronet, but I don't know what Dad would have said. When are we to go?"

"We'll go about seven. We don't need a proper meal this evening after that lunch at the College."

*****

Len Tredwin had made jokes about the beastly bourgeois but his home was respectably middle-class with an arty flavour. The cottage, two miles outside Bridgeminster had oak beams and a log fire, reproductions of modern paintings, chiefly Picassos and several strange pieces of sculpture. One wall of the main room was lined with books; with the exception of the works of Marx and Engels none of them published more than seventy or eighty years ago. Like most men of the Left Len Tredwin hated history. He had, though, a good deal of poetry on his shelves, mostly by Communist Latin-Americans. Mrs. Tredwin was a large, formidable woman with a foreign accent that Richard could not place. He wondered if she could be Russian.

"There's Vodka or Beer," Len Tredwin announced, "both proletarian drinks. No fancy Sherry or Martini in this house!"

Mary did not care for beer and asked if she could try a small vodka. When it came it was not particularly small, but Len explained that it was a lemon-flavoured variety specially imported, that the Comrades in former times reserved for special occasions. Mary sipped cautiously and asked for it to be diluted, while her husband, remembering that he had to drive home, accepted a can of Yorkshire Bitter.

Mrs. Tredwin may have been further to the left than her husband but she had a natural feminine curiosity and questioned the young couple on their marriage, honeymoon and new home. Her husband clearly found the conversation boring and soon found an excuse to lead Richard to a small room at the rear of the cottage dedicated to his famous stamp collection which his visitor had to spend some time admiring.

"I rang Phil Tennant about your yellow stamp question: he collects mainly modern issues. He gave me three names which might fit ... two South American stamps and one from some outlandish place in Africa."

"Where in Africa?"

"The Republic of Gambonia. It used to be called Harrisland in the days of colonial oppression. The 100 Kora stamp is bright yellow Phil says: he's got a specimen."

"Where exactly is Gambonia?"

"Pretty well in the middle of Africa. I looked it up ... here's my Atlas and Directory of Stamp Issuing States. It got it's independence in the sixties ... was run by the first President Dr. M'Tebe for ten years or so: they called him `The Saviour'. Then they had a splendid Marxist government for a few years until that got overthrown; probably undermined by the C.I.A. Since then it has had a succession of régimes and is more or less in a permanent state of civil war. Still manages to issue pretty stamps, though."

Richard studied the page that Tredwin had opened. The map showed that Gambonia was a tropical country with streams that flowed into one of Africa's great rivers. A vast lake was one of its borders.

"Don't you want me to tell you about the South American stamps?"

"You know, I don't think they are likely to tell us anything. You've been very helpful: may I ask you to keep all this quiet for a bit. It may have something to do with my little problem."

"Of course; shall we join the ladies as the quality say."

* * * * * *

Mrs. Tredwin *was* Russian and her name *was* Olga. She had met her husband when he was in Moscow attending a conference organised by the Soviet Lecturers Union, at that time one of the recruiting branches of the K.G.B., and they had been married for more than thirty years. Her husband genuinely thought that she was a True Believer, but being a sensible woman she had never let him suspect that she preferred a middle-class way of life in England to enduring the hardships of an existence in the former Worker's Paradise and had even become an avid reader of newspaper accounts of the affairs of the less respectable members of the Royal Family. Sometimes she wondered whether a restoration of the Romanovs might produce a Russian Princess Di! She had been showing Mary the correct way to drink Vodka and the level in the bottle containing the lemon-flavoured variety had fallen appreciably. The Russian national drink seemed to have no effect on Mrs. Tredwin but Mary looked flushed. Richard noticed that the bottle was labelled over-proof! It was time to take her home.

Mary climbed the stairs to their room unsteadily. When her husband joined her he saw that she had dropped her clothes carelessly on the floor and was already in their bed ... without her night-dress.

"Come on; you're slow. I want to try something Sarah told me about. Her Peter likes it!"

Richard turned out the light and joined her. He had read about such things in books but had not really thought ... but he liked it too!

Chapter 4

On Friday morning Mary had a headache and Richard brought her breakfast in bed. Coffee and toast was all that she required and he boiled himself an egg in the kitchen and admitted Mrs. Barlow the daily help. Mary did not appear and he retired to his study and spent some time examining the file on the missing Mr. Fordham and the list of students who had failed to return to the College from foreign parts. It seemed that Fordham had been academically outstanding. From a minor Public School he had gone up to Cambridge to read Economics and then Law. He had been called to the Bar by the Middle Temple but had not practised, taking up a succession of posts in City financial houses where he had been highly successful. There was no indication as to why he had abandoned these very well paid positions to take the job at Bridgeminster. The file told him nothing else of significance.

The list of absentee students did not seem to help much, either. The two from Hong Kong and Singapore had Chinese names and most of the others African. One of the Africans, domiciled at Capetown, rejoiced in the name of Aloysius Brown. As he considered the list Mary appeared in her dressing-gown.

"Oh dear, that awful drink at the Tredwin's has given me a head. I was silly, wasn't I?"

"It wasn't your fault. It was very strong: I saw the label on the bottle."

They looked at each other in embarrassment but Richard managed to add:

"It was fun though, afterwards: you must tell me what else Sarah told you."

Mary blushed and retreated to the kitchen. She had not yet learned to manage Mrs. Barlow and that good lady was always willing to be paid for hours spent in conversation with her employer.

Later that morning Richard drove to the College. Its car park is vast but it took some time to find a space and the attendant at the entrance had to be persuaded to let him in as he had not obtained the necessary sticker for his windscreen. Eventually he found the bungalow that had been the home of the late Senior Maintenance Officer.

Mrs. Seaforth was fortyish, blonde and still attractive. Her visitor murmured the usual condolences and was invited into a pleasant sitting room the dominant features being a very large television set and a cage containing a brightly coloured parrot. It seemed that the bird did not have the gift of tongues: at regular intervals it uttered a single penetrating squawk, but said nothing constructive.

Mrs. Seaforth was willing to talk:

"I've had the Police here and they asked me lots of questions. Inspector Polk was here again yesterday: he was very kind."

Richard explained that he was not involved with the Police but had been asked to investigate the case of the missing Mr. Fordham. He explained that although there was probably no connection between the two mysteries it might help him to know something of her husband's life.

It was a clumsy excuse but she seemed satisfied.

Mrs. Seaforth, although occasionally tearful, gave her story clearly. She had been away from home on the night of her husband's death, visiting her married daughter who was expecting her first baby.

"Well, not exactly married but you know how it is today."

The Police had not known where she had gone and the first thing she had seen on her return on the Monday morning had been the blue lights of the Police cars flashing in front of the College. It had been a terrible shock.

She had been married for twenty-two years and before coming to Bridgeminster they had lived in London where her husband had been in the Metropolitan Police. He had been about to be promoted Sergeant when he was injured severely during a bank raid. He had jumped in front of the getaway car and had to spend months in hospital. He had been given a commendation and people said he should have had the George Medal. He was, of course, granted a pension and a gratuity and they were lucky enough to find the job at the College.

"Were the bank robbers caught?"

"Oh yes: they had beaten one of the clerks with an iron bar so that he had brain damage. Henry had to give evidence; they sent a lawyer to his bedside in the hospital to take it all down. The robbers got fifteen years, I think."

"Could anyone from those days have had a grudge against your husband?"

"It's more than ten years since he left the Force. Inspector Polk thinks it was someone who broke in to steal computers and Henry disturbed them."

"Did he usually go round the buildings at night? It happened about midnight, I believe."

"He sometimes went to check the heating. They had some trouble with the pipes in B block once. It's not turned on yet; not until half term."

"One last question, Mrs. Seaforth: did your husband know Mr. Fordham ... apart from contact during his work?"

"Well, he wouldn't, would he, him being a Head of Department; ... but he did give Henry a bit of help once."

"How was that?"

"Henry heard that he'd been a lawyer or something like one and he asked him about the cleaners who spoiled my dress."

"Your dress?"

"Ball room: we used to go dancing in spite of Henry being a bit lame because of his injury. When we were first married we won lots of prizes. The cleaners ruined it ... it was a beautiful dress with lovely sequins ... and they said there was small print on the ticket that meant they needn't pay up. Mr. Fordham said that was all so much nonsense and told Henry to go to the Small Claims Court. Henry went and told the manager of the cleaners and it worked out all right. They sent a cheque but not for as much as the dress was worth."

The recollection had made Mrs. Seaforth tearful again and with more sympathetic words Richard made his way to the office of the formidable Miss Penfold. She was not pleased to see him again but handed over a bundle of folders containing Staff Records. He asked for those of lecturers who had been at the College for less than ten years, except those who had arrived in the last two. There were seventy-four of then.

Reluctantly the Assistant Registrar allowed him to occupy a disused office for his investigation and slowly he worked through the files. There were Application Forms, a surprising number of them carelessly filled in and often ill-spelt. There were photocopies of testimonials, those of teachers who had moved frequently from post in post being usually the most flattering, suggesting an eagerness on the part of the writers to see them move on. What did surprise him was the tremendous range of skills to be found in the place and the many different qualifications. The venerable Head of the Building Department's only Diploma was in practical plumbing, while his deputy was a Chartered Architect with a first-class honours degree from Cambridge University. One or two had made claims to qualifications that aroused Richard's detective instincts and one was certainly fraudulent. The applicant had claimed to have been awarded a degree in English Literature from a College which he happened to know had discontinued the course at the time stated! Did no one check, he wondered? It was not until long after that he discovered that the man was one of the most brilliant teachers in the General Studies Department and much loved by his students: their examination results were impressive.

Another discovery was that the qualifications were not always in the subject taught by the lecturer. Sociology was taught by a Bachelor of Divinity, a former Baptist minister who had lost his faith: a lady from the Royal Academy of Dramatic Art and after ten years in Rep, was in charge of the course for Nursery Nurses while a young woman with a degree in Crystallography (whatever that was) from Capetown University was teaching Mathematics. Miss Penfold's own record too, was interesting. She had taken a First in both Mods. and Greats at his own University.

Richard ate his lunch in the students' Cafeteria where a few tables were set aside for members of the staff. It was crowded, littered, noisy, and smelt powerfully of fried foods. It was the first meal he had eaten without Mary's company since their marriage but she had taken the train to Portborough to do some shopping. Lady Smith did not share her husband's lack of interest in clothes and had only just begun to realise the size of the income she now enjoyed from her Marriage Settlement.

Richard confined himself to a single course of pie and chips. They were to dine at home that evening and Mary had banned chips and most other fried foods since beginning her weight-watching campaign. A small man of about fifty, rather corpulent, put down his tray and sat opposite Richard. He was not a weight-watcher: his plate had a double helping of chips, sausages and beans and he had chosen a suet pudding for dessert.

As the man began the pudding stage he spoke.

"I've seen you about but I don't know your name. Which Department are you?"

"I just do a couple of classes ... part-time, you know. I'm doing English Literature for the General Studies. My name's Richard Smith."

The man seemed to become wary. He took a spoonful or two of suet pudding before replying.

"I've heard of you. My name's Graham Parsons - welding in Engineering Department. I read about you getting married in the local paper; India House by the park, isn't it? Lovely gates you've got; I passed it the other day and saw that you've had them redone: beautiful. You couldn't get ironwork like that done today."

"I'm glad you approve."

"I read something else about you. I suppose that you're here because of Harry Seaforth's murder: nasty business."

"Very; but you're quite wrong. Just doing a bit of teaching to keep my hand in."

Parsons smiled in obvious disbelief.

"You found the men who killed old Colonel Wainwright. He fined me once for careless driving when he was on the Bench."

"Bad luck."

The teacher of welding finished his pudding and stood to go.

"I wouldn't have coffee here if I was you. It's better in the staff room. Have you found it yet?"

"I'll come with you."

They walked through a long corridor to the entrance hall where the body of the caretaker had been found and then to the staircase that led to the staff room. At the foot Graham Parsons turned and stopped.

"Come and see me when my class finishes. Three-thirty in Workshop 17B: I ought to tell you something."

They climbed the stairs to the staff room and drank their coffee, talking the while of ornamental iron-work.

Richard spent the next two hours in the tiny room assigned him and finished the last of the staff dossiers.

He made copious notes but made no important discoveries and at 3.30 made his way to the workshop area. The welding shop was empty except for a single figure in a grubby white coat of the sort that the engineering teachers generally wore. The man looked up as Richard entered but did not speak and almost immediately Graham Parsons emerged from a door in the corner of the work-shop, behind which was the hiding place ... a former tool store ... where the welding staff made themselves comfortable. There were three battered chairs and a small table, a calendar with a picture of a scantily clad beauty, an electric kettle and an array of partly washed mugs. The kettle was steaming cheerfully as they entered the den and Parsons took teabags from a tin on the table.

"Cuppa?" he asked. He went to the door and shouted, "Ted, tea up," but Ted did not appear.

They sipped the strong tea for some minutes and Richard waited for the welder to begin. Eventually, he spoke.

"I don't want to get mixed up in anything. I'm trying for early retirement and I don't want to upset the Sergeant Major."

"The Sergeant Major?"

"We call him that in this department: Doctor Floodgate."

Richard wondered whether each Department had a name for the Principal. He smiled and waited.

"I didn't want to go to the Police. I suppose you're well in with them and could pass it on without mentioning my name."

"If it's about the murder you ought to tell them. I was telling the truth when I said that I was not concerned with that ... except in curiosity, naturally. I was asked to look into something else ... not criminal at all."

"I'll have to risk it. I liked Harry Seaforth."

"What do you know?"

The welding lecturer drank his tea rather noisily.

"Look, most of us engineers do a few little jobs on the side. Someone wants a bit of metal work done ... a barbecue, say or something of the sort. Perhaps just a lawn mower that wants repairing. A bottle of whisky, maybe or a few quid. Strictly against the rules, but ... the old Principal never worried about it ... I made him a trailer for a boat his kids had ... but this man ... but he doesn't ask too many questions. Of course Harry Seaforth had to know because sometimes the work had to be done when the College was officially closed. I've done some jobs for him at times ... I made that stand for the bird-cage in his living room."

"I saw it: a nice bit of work."

"Well, I came in to College on the Sunday morning ... making up some engine bearers for a boat belonging to a friend. He's changing over to Diesel. I finished the job in the afternoon: I brought a few sandwiches with me so I didn't go home for lunch. I tidied up and went home about four ..."

"Why ...?"

"No, nothing special happened: but that was the afternoon before Harry was killed."

"Yes, I thought you'd tell me that."

"When I got in on the Monday morning ... after getting past all those policemen ... they closed the College, you know ... I came in here ... and someone had been doing some welding since I left."

"Strange, how did you know?"

"When I finished there were three welding rods left. I didn't bother to put them back in the store so I left them on the bench. In the morning there were only two."

"Are you sure?"

"Definitely: there were three when I left. There was something else, too: there was a slight smell of paint. We don't use paint in here much."

"Could someone on the staff have come in?"

"There's only Ted who does welding here. I asked him and he hadn't."

"May I see the workshop?"

The room was some forty foot by twenty with a number of benches and small cubicles in which welding equipment was laid out. There were no students present and the figure in the white coat, presumably Ted, had disappeared. Numerous notices on the walls warned both staff and pupils of the dangers they faced and gave instructions for reviving the victims of electric shock or asphyxiation. At the far end of the shop were double doors large enough to admit a vehicle.

"Who has keys?"

"You don't know this place. Keys are always getting lost. Harry Seaforth had a full set and Ted Morgan and I have keys to the doors in this section. We keep all the tools locked up: students are always trying to nick them."

Richard thought for a moment and then replied.

"Look, Len, I think I ought to tell my policeman friend about your story. I'll ask him to keep you out of it if it's possible: he's a sensible chap. By the way, are there any other teachers who can do welding?"

"Most of the engineers would know how to do simple work. I have a class for do-it-yourself welders on Tuesday evenings. I've got a bank manager, a parson and a dentist in it."

Richard left the College at about four-fifteen and returned home. Mary had not returned from her shopping trip and her husband spent some time in thought. Eventually he rang Inspector Polk at the Station.

"Jim, Richard here. Can you come round this evening: about eight, perhaps?"

"What have you been up to?"

"Nothing much: just one or two little facts."

"Found that teacher that's run away to sea?"

"Not yet, see you later."

* * * * *

Mary returned at five-thirty with a new winter coat that Richard did not much care for but he was already an experienced enough husband to dissemble a little. He was more enthusiastic about the underwear she had bought and wondered if it was on the recommendation of his Canadian sister-in-law. Several pieces were of an advanced nature!

* * * * *

They sat in the Parlour ... the name had stuck, to await James Polk's arrival.

Polk was not cheerful. Richard had heard of manic-depressives and thought it possible that the detective came into that category, for at times he could be wildly elated ... usually when he imagined that he had made a great hit in one of the Bridgeminster Theatre Club's productions. Richard passed him the whisky bottle and he poured himself his usual treble.

"Bad day, Jim?"

Polk had had a very bad one. A gang of teenage muggers and car thieves had been apprehended and he had spent the day wading through a pile of reports from a variety of Social Workers. They had been very lengthy.

"And what on earth is the good of all that stuff, I can't imagine. A waste of public money."

"For once I agree with you, Jim. Have I ever told you my theory about jobs like that?" Mary gave a faint groan; she had heard it already. Polk, though, was quite prepared to listen to his friend laying down the law if his glass was kept filled.

"Go on," he said.

"It would make a splendid subject for a thesis, Jim, or a learned work entitled ... say ... `Therapeutic Occupations for the Unemployable."

You see, in every age there has to be a profession that will support people who could never be usefully employed but who would be a nuisance to Society if they were entirely idle. In the Middle Ages the Church maintained thousands of Monks, Nuns, Friars, Exorcists and I don't know what: in the eighteenth century elaborately uniformed soldiers marched and counter-marched and seldom did much damage when they fought each other. Now, for the last hundred years or so it has been Education; armies of teachers, professors, lecturers; casting imaginary pearls before real swine, as they say. But you see, Jim, they've been rumbled; people are beginning to realise that few of them actually teach anything ... anything worth learning, that is.

"So, a new profession has to arise and I think that it will be Social Work. Just the job for not very intelligent, not very hard working busybodies. There's a thesis for you! I'm sorry you had a tough day, though."

"I'll say it was. And then there's this Seaforth case. Why is it that I keep getting cases with nothing to go on. There he was, shot in the middle of the night when he ought to have been in bed. His wife away too, so no info on his movements that day. Not even a bullet: it went right through him and out through a window ... heavy calibre; made a horrible mess ... I prefer nice tidy corpses."

"Was he shot from the front?"

"The forensic boys say so: I can't imagine how they can tell."

"No sign of a struggle?"

"He wouldn't have struggled with that hole in him."

"Nothing stolen from the College?"

"Not that they can tell. Mind you I don't think they know what they've got there. You get a warehouse break-in and they have a list all ready for you ... for the insurance claim, naturally. Here it's public property so no one bothers."

Richard, the ex-teacher, knew all about waste in Education.

"It looks as if he might have known the killer. He was an ex-policeman: might he have recognised the intruder ... or could it be a criminal who had a grudge against him?"

"You've been looking into my case: I knew you would;" Polk sounded resigned. "Of course we know his background. He was a well thought of cop when he was in the Met. His evidence helped to put that Thornton Heath gang away. They've been out of prison four or five years now: I checked. They wouldn't have waited that long, would they?"

Polk went on to describe the difficult attitude of his Superintendent, who wanted quick results. 'POLICE BAFFLED' was not a head-line that the Force likes to see.

It was not until he had taken another helping of The Macallan that he remembered to ask about Richard's case.

"How's the case of the Missing Teacher going? I heard you upset that Registrar lady. One of my D.C.s went to look through her Staff Records on Seaforth for the second time and she flew off the handle. Really scared him!"

"No, nothing's turned up, really. Except ... well you know my methods, as the man said."

"I know: you make up little fairy stories with all the bits you've found out and when you've got a really nice one ... hey presto, the case is solved. You ought to go and teach them at the Police College!"

Mary looked rather alarmed: she had not yet learned the limits of her husband's tolerance.

"Don't you think the two cases are connected? I do," she asked.

"We never rule out any possibilities, but I don't see it myself. Fordham had gone off long before this killing."

Mary persisted: "Yes, but why did he go?"

"Do you know how many people go off like that ... hundreds. The Salvation Army has a whole department trying to trace them. Reasons? Sex, Money, Curiosity or just plain boredom. Escaping from married life is the most common," he added with a grin.

"And what about that letter the Principal got?" Mary was not going to give up.

"You ought to have shown me that, you know. I heard about it from Floodgate. He's a careful fellow, too; he'd made a photo-copy. I'll take the original, though and give it to Forensic. It'll have your dabs all over it, I suppose."

"No it won't: when he gave it to me I handled it by one corner and afterwards folded it with a pair of tweezers."

Polk looked slightly impressed.

"You're learning," he commented, "but it won't tell us anything: that sort of letter never does."

Chapter 5

During the weeks before the half-term break there were
no developments in the matter of the missing Mr. Fordham
or Inspector Polk's murder inquiries. Richard gave his
class the Wife of Bath's Tale (which bored them) and
desperately tried them with More's Utopia. That work
almost provoked them to rebellion, so, skipping
Shakespeare, Spenser and the Elizabethans generally ...
they had all suffered from The Bard at school ... he moved
on to a gory Jacobean play with much rape, matricide and
incest. They liked that very much. At the end of October
he was sent the monthly cheque for £81.24p for his efforts.

At the half-term they drove to Dorset for a short break
holiday advertised in the Daily Telegraph. The place was
comfortable but the food uninspiring. Mary was fond of
the works of Thomas Hardy, an author that her husband
found depressing, but he dutifully accompanied her to
the proper places to visit. The only happening to disturb
his peace of mind was Mary's declaration that she believed
herself to be pregnant. For three days she was blissfully
happy and even visited the Bridgeminster branch of
Babycare. It was a false alarm and Richard's relief was
somewhat marred by her evident disappointment. Several
days passed before he found the courage to bring up the
subject.

"I thought you were going to go to the Clinic when we
got back."

"Would you mind if I didn't? I'm twenty-four and
you're twenty-nine: and you did say you wanted an heir."

"Did I? Well ..." Richard was too much in love to deny
her anything, but it was an awesome prospect. He thought
twenty-nine much too young to become a father.

On the first Monday after the half-term holiday Richard
and Mary took the 9.12 train to London, she to the West

End shops and he to call on Mr. Goldman of the firm of Lawrence and Latham, Stockbrokers. In the summer they had advised him to retain a large holding in Outback Hotels Ltd. that his late Australian uncle had acquired in a careless moment. The firm had gone into liquidation and Richard had lost more than half a million. On the other hand they had advised him to buy United Fruit Plantations and he had made a capital gain (before tax) of a million and a quarter. Perhaps in remorse because of the hotel fiasco Mr. Goldman produced a better sherry than usual from the cupboard behind his desk. They talked about stocks and shares for half an hour, Mr. Goldman with the enthusiasm of a man whose work was the only interest in his life and Richard tried not to sound bored.

Casually as he prepared to leave, Richard put a question.

"By the way, Mr. Goldman, I suppose you know a great many people in the City. Have you ever met an Edward Fordham? He was in a Merchant Bank, or something of the sort until about three or four years ago."

"Fordham; Edward Fordham, no I don't think so. I knew a Philip Fordham years ago but he's dead now. He pressed a button on his desk and his middle-aged secretary appeared instantly. Mr. Goldman was much too wide awake to entrust his confidential affairs to a popsie."

"Miss Willingham, do we know an Edward Fordham? ... was in a Merchant Bank, Sir Richard thinks."

"Oh yes, Mr. Goldman, and his brother. He was with Gurney and Mason and before that with Overbury's. His brother runs B.L.W."

Miss Willingham had a photographic memory.

"Thanks Maisie; I remember the chap now. Can't think where I met him, though. Brainy chap, if I've got the right one. Not always an advantage in the City, Sir Richard: greed and low cunning much more important."

As stockbrokers go Mr. Goldman was not actually very greedy: the game was what he enjoyed.

"Can you tell me anything about the man? You see he has disappeared and I've been asked to investigate the matter. There is nothing criminal involved, I can assure you, but his ... er ... friends are worried."

"I knew you were a sort of detective."

"Well, `sort of' is about the right description."

"He hasn't absconded, then?"

"No, but treat this as confidential ..."

Richard gave the stockbroker a concise account of the strange disappearance of the Head of the Business Studies Department, omitting any mention of the murder. Mr. Goldman seized on the point that Richard had been worrying.

"How much was he earning in that job?"

"About £35,000, I understand. Perhaps a little more."

"He'd have been making four times that with Gurney and Mason; plus bonuses which would have been considerable."

"Really, as much as that?"

"Oh, yes; they're a good firm." Mr. Goldman's manner changed.

"Wait a minute, Sir, Richard, you said there was nothing criminal. I've just remembered reading in the Mail. There was a murder in a College at Bridgeminster a few weeks ago. Was it the same one?"

"Yes, it was. The Police are convinced that there was no connection with Fordham's disappearance."

"Odd coincidence, though."

Mr. Goldman had become more wary and Richard thought it time to go.

"Last question, Mr. Goldman; what is B.L.W.?"

"Birmingham Light Weapons. They make all sorts of guns and things. They got a Queen's Award for exports. You could do worse than buy their shares."

"I'll think about it: thankyou Mr. Goldman, you've been very helpful."

On the way home Mary described her purchases but Richard did not give them the attention they deserved. They arrived back at India House in time for a supper from the deep-freeze and soon after Mary got her husband to bed with a purposeful look in her eyes. She had been studying a pamphlet entitled 'What You Ought to Know About the Safe Period' and had worked out that this Monday was not one!

The English Literature class on Tuesday was not looking forward to 'Paradise Lost'. They thought it sounded like the 'R.E.' which had been administered in forty minute packages throughout their school careers. Those that paid attention thought Lucifer a rather fine fellow, and wondered why the Almighty had such a down on him.

After the class Richard walked to the small bungalow behind the gymnasium ... or 'Sports Hall' as it was now named and called on Mrs. Seaforth. Since his last visit she seemed to have begun to recover from her loss, offered him tea and talked about her plans for the future. The Council were going to give her a flat. Dr. Floodgate had used all his influence to get her one on the better of the two Bridgeminster estates; the other was well known for crime and vandalism and few of the tenants paid their rent regularly, the District Councils rent account showing a deficiency of almost two million pounds. She talked on ... she was clearly lonely, now ... and it was some time before Richard found the opportunity to question her.

"I wanted to ask you a couple of questions, Mrs. Seaforth. About your life before your sad loss."

"Do call me Megan, Sir Richard."

"Megan, that's a Welsh name."

"My mother was from Llanelli"; she pronounced the name correctly.

"First; did you have a car?"

"Oh yes, an Astra. It's by the side of the house: there's no garage. I can't drive so I'll have to get rid of it. Thank goodness, the H.P. is paid off."

"So, if your husband went somewhere in the car people would know he was away?"

"Yes."

"Then it was by the house the night he was ... the night it happened."

"No, it wasn't. He put it in Tucker's Garage to have the brakes done and they hadn't finished it by Saturday: Henry was very cross. Mr. Bannister in the Motor Engineering Section usually gets that sort of job done for Staff Members but he was away on a course that week."

Richard considered for a few moments.

"Did you often go away at weekends?"

"Oh, yes. We wouldn't go on Saturday because most of the cleaners were in. We'd go on Sunday morning and come back early on Monday. Ken Archer ... he's Deputy Maintenance Officer, would be in charge until Henry got back."

"Where did you go?"

"To his Mum's. She's on her own since my father-in-law died and we'd get there for Sunday lunch and stay overnight."

"Where does she live?"

"Bishopsgate."

Bishopsgate is some sixty miles from Bridgeminster.

"So you went most weekends?"

"Henry was very fond of his Mum." Megan Seaforth made this statement in a tone that suggested that she was not quite so affectionate towards her mother-in-law.

Richard rose to leave.

"By the way, did your husband usually go to bed early?"

"He did, always. I sometimes stayed up to watch T.V."

"You have been very helpful, Megan. One thing more, though: do you mind if I ask you if you're all right for money ... if I could help in any way ... perhaps ...?"

"I'm going to get a pension, Sir Richard and Henry paid in an Insurance for me. I shall be all right, I think."

She again looked weepy.

"Would you take this, though. It will help with all the expenses of moving ... and I've just remembered, too, that there's a lot of furniture in the flat I lived in before I got married, and a cooker and a washing machine too. If you would like to help yourself, do. I shall be selling the flat now."

Richard had taken from his pocket a thick envelope. He had called at the bank on his way to the College and it contained a substantial sum in banknotes.

Megan Seaforth wept again and her 'thankyous' were sincere but hardly coherent.

It was now about four o'clock and there were other calls to be made. Amid the squalor of the staff room of the General Studies Department Richard sought the Senior Lecturer in Modern Languages. All the languages taught in that Department were modern, there being no demand for the Classics. French, Spanish, Russian and German were on the curriculum for full-time students and many other tongues were offered by part-time teachers to evening class clients. They had even found a charming Japanese lady, married to an Englishman, who had, to the Senior Lecturer's surprise, managed to keep her lessons in that difficult language going for three years. They referred to her as 'the Geisha Girl'!

Andrew Campbell was one of the few members of the staff not to be slightly in awe of the Baronet part-time teacher. Not many of the lecturers were graduates of the older universities. Mr. Campbell was a Balliol man and had no respect for men from Lazarus. Moreover he thought that the course the University of Oxford provided in English Literature was a soft option. He was polite, but not enthusiastic when asked for information about the linguistic abilities of his team.

"What I want to know, Mr. Campbell, is whether you have a lecturer with knowledge of at least three languages; French, Portuguese and ... Swahili. Of course, English too."

Campbell looked surprised. He was an intelligent man and grasped the point instantly.

"That would be someone who had lived in Africa; East Africa, I would guess."

"Exactly."

"We've got three graduates in French, and one I know did Portuguese as a subsidiary: not fluent in it though. As to Swahili I would think it unlikely. A good linguist might pick up a bit on a package tour: I learned some Serbo-Croat in Yugo-Slavia. I suppose this is all to do with your detective business."

"Yes, I must ask you to be discreet. The Principal has asked me to look into the matter of Mr. Fordham's disappearance."

"I can't say I approve. Breach of contract is not a criminal offence, is it? You enjoy this sort of thing, do you?"

Richard was embarrassed by the man's attitude and made no reply.

"I'll make inquiries and let you know, Sir Richard." There was to be no familiar use of Christian names by Mr. Campbell.

Before leaving the College there was another duty to be done.

In all his twenty-nine years no-one except his Mother had told him that he needed a haircut. Unlike most of his contemporaries he had never taken much interest in the styling of his hair: in fact it could not be said to have any style at all and his 'short back and sides' would have satisfied any Sergeant-Major had he chosen a military career. Nevertheless at breakfast that morning Mary had said, "You need a hair-cut."

"I don't think I have time today."

"You can get it done at the College. They do ladies and gents' hairdressing in the training salons. Jane Carpenter had a perm there and it looks quite nice. She says her husband gets his hair cut for 50p."

" It's a consideration."

The Department of the College that trains Hairdressers and Beauty therapists is a busy one. At the reception desk an incredibly smart female trainee consulted her book and found that Richard could have his hair done immediately if he went to Mr. Pyle's class in D Salon: they were doing Gents Hairdressing today.

Mr. Pyle was Lecturer in charge of part-time students ... most of them ladies of a certain age thinking of taking up a new career. It might be that he did at times do something as restful as lecture, but on this day he was much more active. There were a dozen chairs, in each of which sat an old-age pensioner enjoying a cut-price hair-cut.

Mr. Pyle was in his thirties, very slim and athletic looking. He looked fit enough for the Centre Court at Wimbledon but Richard heard later that he was an enthusiastic mid-field player for his local football team.

By each chair an earnest would-be hairdresser was snipping cautiously at the grey locks of a Senior Citizen, while Mr. Pyle dashed from one to the other giving a word of advice here and an admonition there. Sometimes he would take the scissors and demonstrate: he was never still. His pupils obviously loved him. They called him 'Phil' and he knew all their Christian names. Richard wondered how he preserved discipline with such informality: he, himself had always addressed his College students as 'Mr.' and 'Miss' (to their consternation), and he had expected them to call him 'Sir Richard'.

A College haircut is well worth 50p. but it can be rather slow. The middle aged lady dealing with Richard's hair seemed to cut one hair at a time and once she jabbed her sitter painfully with the point of her scissors. The eagle-eye of Mr. Pyle must have observed this for he took over the work.

"I'll finish this, Sandra: you watch."

Sandra, who had been close to tears, withdrew and the hand of the master took the scissors.

"You're Sir Richard Smith. I've seen you about."

"Do call me Richard: you're Philip Pyle, I think."

Pyle was not a garrulous barber. Richard exchanged a few words with him until the use of the electric clippers made it difficult, but as he paid his fifty pence to the girl in charge of the till Pyle returned.

"Anytime you want a haircut I can fit you in. Priority to Staff, you know."

"Thanks; good of you to step in and finish me off. The lady was drooping a bit!"

"Well your hair isn't exactly a challenge. Grow it a bit longer and we can do something interesting with it."

The last thing Sir Richard wanted was interesting hair. He took a chance.

"Did Edward Fordham have his hair done here?"

"He was used to West End hairdressers: he only came once; just before he left, actually. Brenda over there gave him a trim."

"Was he acting normally?"

"Oh, yes. He didn't talk much: said he was getting a bit grey and asked me about hair dying."

"Was he getting grey?"

"Hardly at all. A touch here and there. I recommended him to try `Tintex'. You're not needing dye yet ... but you are thinning a bit on top. Don't waste your money on hair restorers; none of them work."

* * * * *

Mary had prepared an evening meal more lavish than usual. M. Lebel had given her his recipe for Lobster Thermidor and, (though appalled at it's cost) she had bought a large specimen and prepared the dish with great care. There was a bottle of the Sancerre and a rich ready-made dessert from Waitrose. It was not that she was consciously trying to put her husband in the right mood but her careful calculations had shown her that Tuesday was also an auspicious day. It is better to leave nothing to chance.

After dinner, however, he wanted to talk about the case.

"Whoever got into that welding shop on the night of the murder would have thought that Seaforth was away. His car was not in it's usual parking space and his wife had gone to her daughter's."

"Is the man sure somebody worked there?"

"He says he is: what is a welding rod?"

"I don't know."

Mary poured the coffee and looked disapproving as her husband reached for the bottle of Benedictine.

"Do you think you ought to have a liqueur; you had more than half the bottle of wine. It'll make you sleepy."

"Well, we're going to bed presently."

"Only a small one, then."

Mary prepared herself for more direct methods but Richard had another question.

"I haven't got a good atlas. Is there one among your books?"

Mary's box of books had not yet been found shelves.

"I've got a big atlas: I did A level Geography ... and got a Grade A."

"Clever old you: where is it?"

"You don't want it tonight, do you? It would take a bit of finding."

Richard eventually got the message and they went to bed.

* * * * *

Mary went off to her cookery class, perfectly satisfied with the previous night's happenings. Before she left she had found the rather battered atlas and looking through her books Richard discovered that she had a large work on Commercial Geography, not too out of date. He took them to his study but did not immediately examine them. He left the house and walked the short distance to Bridgeminster's shopping centre and called at Cringle's Estate Agency, where the red-nosed proprietor welcomed him with enthusiasm.

"Sir Richard; are you going to tell me that your cousin wants to see the house I showed you?"

"My Aunt, actually, Mr. Cringle," ... when being economical with the truth it is important to remember what one has said ... "unfortunately she has not been well, but we hope to have her with us for Christmas. She asked me to get the measurements of the rooms. I've brought a tape measure."

Mr. Cringle was too experienced an Agent to believe Richard's story: moreover he had picked up some gossip about his client's detective work. Richard went on quickly.

"I have some other work for you. I own a leasehold flat in Bridgeminster that I lived in before I married; Downview Mansions, actually. Would you like to put it on your books: I will give you the sole agency."

Flats in that block are not high-priced, but they sell quickly. Mr. Cringle cheered up; it would be one more towards his target for the year.

"Of course, Sir Richard. Perhaps you will tell me when I can come round to measure up."

"I'll do better than that. Here is a set of keys. There is still some furniture there but I am disposing of that. Can we go to the house you showed me, now?"

Some weeks had passed since Richard had visited the house on the Larkhill Estate. There were dead leaves on the path and the garden had not been tidied for the winter. More letters lay in the hall and Cringle again picked them up and pocketed them. Richard did not see any with bright yellow foreign stamps. This time the Agent did not accompany him as he went round the house with tape measure and note-book, but sat in a chair in the lounge. It is difficult to search a house without making a noise but he was able to open one or two drawers and cupboards. The larder shelves still carried jars and containers of non-perishable foods; the previous occupants had drunk Nestles' Blend 37 instant coffee, used lemon scented washing-up liquid and consumed Waitrose 'own brand' cracker biscuits. The drinks cabinet contained only bottles of dry and medium sherry and a rather strange shaped bottle of Dutch Schnapps. There was something different about the bookshelves. The works on golfing remained;

the travel books had been removed. Upstairs the very heavy curtains had been half drawn and the room was dark. Richard pressed a light switch and the light came on. The previous occupants had neglected to turn off the current at the mains.

Mr. Cringle was tapping his foot impatiently when Richard rejoined him.

"Well, Mr. Cringle, that all seems very satisfactory."

Richard announced in what he imagined were the tones of an eager buyer. "I will let my Aunt have all the details and I'm sure she will be interested."

As they left the house he noticed a curtain lifted in a ground floor window of the next-door residence and a thin female face watching their departure.

It was still only 10:30 a.m. and Richard returned to India House. He had been instructed to prepare a simple lunch ... it was Mrs. Barlow's day off ... and had decided on a couple of chops from the deepfreeze, mashed potatoes ... chips were still banned ... and frozen peas. Mary's class were doing puddings this week and she hoped to have something interesting to bring home. There was no need to start work for another forty minutes or so; he made himself a mug of tea and sat down with the newspaper.

GAMBONIAN REBELS ADVANCE ON CAPITAL

was the headline. Apparently that tortured country's civil war was coming to a gory end. Thousands of refugees were attempting to flee the country; there had been massacres of supporters of the Government that had fallen into rebel hands: the word 'genocide' was being used. The C.P.L. (Campaign for Peace and Liberty) were not keen to take prisoners. The war had been going on in a desultory fashion for a long time but the report stated that in the last year or so the insurgents had received large supplies of modern weapons and had even acquired a number of hand-held missiles capable of shooting down the Government jets. The U.N. was trying to mediate.

Richard put the paper down and went to the kitchen to peel potatoes. He was not good at peeling: when he had got the skin off there never seemed to be much potato left. He did some more and put them on to boil. He took two chops from the deep-freeze and placed them in the micro-wave, setting it at 'Defrost'. The frozen peas could wait. Then he returned to his study and opened Mary's atlas at the map of Central Africa.

Gambonia (formerly Harrisland), seemed designed for guerilla warfare. Its eastern region bordering the great lake was shown as dense rain forest. There was a mountainous district in the North and marshes lay on each side of the rivers. The high ground in the West contained several extinct volcanoes. It was a land-locked country and few roads and railways were shown. Richard turned to Mary's geography text-book where there was a short description of the economic resources of the country. It was said to be 'undeveloped' but probably with considerable potential. Its principal exports had been tropical timber, cocoa beans and bananas, but at that date (1975) prospecting was going on for oil and minerals. It was believed that gold had once been mined in the Northern region, but only in small quantities.

A man should not combine criminal investigation and cookery. When Richard remembered the potatoes they had disintegrated in the saucepan and the resulting mashed potato looked very watery. If the husband's dish was a failure the wife's pudding from the cookery class was a great success. The class had not been without excitement. Mr. Blenkinsopp, the only male member had cut his finger badly while slicing apples, and three widows, each one claiming to have a first-class certificate from the Red Cross competed for the privilege of bandaging it. They were outbid by a very elderly spinster, who was said to have been the first nursing sister to wade ashore on the Normandy beaches in 1944. This event had prevented Mary from getting any more information about Henry Seaforth from the academic bachelor.

* * * * *

"Fordham's disappearance has something to do with the Dark Continent," Richard argued after lunch. "The letter, probably from Africa, the books on the shelves that have now disappeared; the students that have not returned: there are too many coincidences. Perhaps he's gone to Africa."

"You could check with the Travel Agents."

"The Police could: they wouldn't tell us anything. That's the difficulty, not being official."

"Ask Jim Polk to see them."

"No, not yet: he's not taking it seriously, anyway."

"I still think it has something to do with the murder."

"So do I, now ... but there's no evidence for it. I know ... there is someone we can talk to."

"Who?"

"When I left the Fordham house there was someone watching us from the house next door: a rather inquisitive lady. She might know something of the former inhabitants. Where's that copy of the electoral roll?"

Richard had obtained one at the beginning of the investigation to avoid having to return to the ferocious Miss Penfold to ask for the addresses of staff members. It showed that No. 22 was occupied by Gartside; Eleanor, J., a widow or a spinster, no doubt.

"I think you had better come with me. A lady living alone might be nervous of male callers. We'll go in the car."

Gartside; Eleanor J., was an imposing figure. She looked rather like the headmistress of St. Trinian's, portrayed by the late Mr. Alastair Sim. In fact she was formerly of that profession, but of a perfectly respectable Church of England school.

Richard used the well-tried story. They were looking for a house for an elderly Aunt and had been shown Number 20. They would like to know about the estate; the neighbours, particularly. Aunt Jane was a rather nervous person and hated noise: also was there much traffic because she had three cats? Richard had observed a handsome Persian on the window ledge. Miss Gartside looked them up and down carefully. Richard had used his title in introducing himself and she seemed satisfied that her visitors were genuine.

"Come in, Sir Richard. I think I read about your wedding in the local paper. It was at St. Michael's wasn't it? I used to worship there until Canon Bassett started these new services. He wanted us to clap our hands and that sort of thing. Would you and Lady Smith like a cup of tea?"

Detectives have to accept every offer of tea and it was served with considerable ceremony. It took a while to get Miss Gartside to discuss the neighbours, but when she did she was a mine of information.

"I didn't know Mr. Fordham or his wife at all well. They kept themselves to themselves, you know. He was a lecturer at the College but I don't think his wife worked. She was a lot younger than he was and she was often away. I said to him once, "I haven't seen your wife for some time", and he said that she had to go and look after her mother who was ill. She'd take his car when she went off and he'd walk to work."

"I think I've met his wife. Very fair hair, if I remember correctly."

"Oh no, Sir Richard, reddish. She was quite slim."

"Did they have many visitors?"

"Hardly any; only the young lady who sometimes came at weekends. I think she may have been his wife's sister because there was a resemblance, only she had dark hair. She's been back since they went away: they must have given here the key of the house."

"I think I saw a car parked on their drive. A Mini I think."

"I'm afraid I don't know about cars. The young lady had a white one."

"It must be nice to have quiet people living next door," Mary put in, "my husband's Aunt leads a very quiet life."

"Oh, it is: I'm sure your Aunt will be the right sort of neighbour: and a cat lover, too ..."

Miss Gartside looked fondly at her Persian.

"... but I must say I never had any trouble with the Fordhams ... except once when they upset my television."

"Your television?"

"Yes: he had some sort of gadget that was making scratches on my screen. I asked the man from the Radio Shop to come and he said it was interference from a local source. I went round and Mr. Fordham was very nice about it: he said he'd check everything and sure enough it stopped. I do like to see the news and Panorama."

Miss Gartside had a good deal to say about other neighbours but no more about the missing Mr. Fordham or the young lady with the key. She began to question them about the imaginary Aunt and as they had not agreed together about her character, Mary avoided questions by explaining that Aunt Jane had not been able to come to their wedding because of her health. Richard's imagination worked overtime. They got away at last.

"I do hope your Aunt takes the house, Sir Richard. Is she Lady Smith, too?"

"Oh, no, Miss Gartside. Just Miss Jane Smith, O.B.E. A retired headmistress like yourself."

Richard had been about to give himself an Aunt Muriel, but remembered the choice of names in time. However he had made a mistake. Miss Gartside showed rather less enthusiasm at the prospect of a retired headmistress as neighbour. Two of a trade seldom agree.

They drove away. "Why the O.B.E.?" Mary asked.

"Just to add verisimilitude to a bald and unconvincing ..."

"You really must drop the Victorian humour: I suppose it's middle-age! I was watching your face while she was talking: it must be married life; I can sometimes guess what you're thinking."

"A dangerous gift. What was I thinking?"

"When she said all that about her television not working properly. You didn't seem surprised."

"Did you think I was surprised when she told us about the young woman in the Mini?"

"No: she must have been the one who took away the books. Why didn't she take away the letters that had been delivered: you said Cringle took them. Did you think it odd that she wore a hat? Few girls do today: I've only got one."

"True; you know Mary, taking all the facts into consideration, I'm pretty sure there was something criminal going on in that College and that Fordham was involved. Also it's fairly certain that the murder is connected with it. I've been wondering whether we shouldn't do more to persuade Jim Polk to see it. In that Thelwell case I left telling him rather late. It could have been fatal for us."

Mary shuddered as she remembered the day of their incredible escape ... and also of their engagement.

"What sort of crime, though?"

"That's the point. Look, Dr. Floodgate said something to me the day I saw him at the College. He said that on his staff you could find an expert in almost any field. Now, suppose you had some complicated criminal scheme in your mind that would need many different skills ... you could recruit all the people you needed."

"If there were enough criminal types among them."

"What if it was not very criminal ... perhaps technically a crime but not very wicked? I've got something at the back of my mind but it's not clear yet. Don't forget, too, that teachers are not very well paid. There must be a lot of money involved, somewhere."

That evening they sat up late going over the case. Mary had looked at her calculations again and found no urgent reason to get her husband to bed. She even made no protest when he poured himself a second drink. It was Mary, though who had a new idea.

"You haven't done anything about those students?"

"Students? My class?"

"No, the ones who didn't come back from Africa."

"You're right, but what can I do about them?"

"There might be students there now who knew some of them."

"Difficult: there's only one foreign student in my class but he's an Arab. They say he's a mathematical genius but I don't think he understands a word of my lectures."

"We must have your class round here for a little party. Before Christmas, say ... I'm longing to meet them. I know!"

Mary stopped suddenly.

"Know what?"

"The Reverend Anthea. She runs a sort of club for overseas students at the Rectory. You could go along and meet them and find one who knew an absentee."

It was Richard's turn to shudder.

"Couldn't you go? I don't think she likes me much."
"That's why you've got to go. I think she rather likes me!"

"Well, it's an idea. I'll ring her up to-morrow."

"Think of a good lie. I know; you are planning a Safari holiday in Africa and would like to get to know the background. They'll know you can afford a Safari."

"I can't think of anything more boring.

"Oh, I think I'd rather enjoy one. Lions roaring in the night and hyenas".

Richard agreed that her idea was a good one but his last words before going to bed were ...

"I think I shall talk to Jim Polk soon."

Chapter 6

St. Michael's Rectory is a vast red brick building, put up in late Victorian times when a clergyman with a good living could employ half a dozen servants to wait on his large family. Canon Bassett and his wife occupied a small part of it; the rest being devoted to parish purposes.

The Reverend Ms. Spofforth had, with Christian forgiveness, borne no grudge against Sir Richard for having arranged his wedding on her afternoon off and denying her the opportunity to cheer her girls in the first football game of the season: they had been defeated 7-1. However she did not approve of titles nor of inherited wealth and it took a little persuasion to get her to introduce Richard to the members of her club. There were four or five from India, two from Ceylon, a Coptic Egyptian and the rest from Africa. All claimed to be Christians and there could have been no Moslems among them for the Rev. Anthea had provided ham sandwiches.

There was table tennis, darts and card games and in the smaller of the two rooms there was a video film showing. Richard attempted to circulate: it was not easy.

The Copt was working for A levels and hoped to read architecture at an English University. Impressed by Richard's title he began a plea on behalf of his two brothers. Would Sir Richard use all his influence to help his two brothers to join him in England? The two from Ceylon had a grievance against the College authorities. They, too, were in A level classes but had been denied admission to the course of their choice. Would the baronet try to persuade the Principal? The Indians had no complaints but wanted to talk about cricket: their Test Team was to tour England next season. All these students were male: the Africans were a mixed group and were occupied with chatting up their female compatriots. One of them seemed to have failed to attract such company and was sitting in a corner reading a motoring magazine. He was apparently of Asian origin and looked intelligent.

His name was Iskander (Richard never managed to pronounce his surname) and he came from Uganda. His family had fled from the persecution of Idi Amin but had prospered in England and only returned to Africa after the fall of that dictator. Prudently, they had retained business interests in England. Knowing that Uganda was close to Gambonia, Richard asked him if he had ever visited that strife-torn land. Iskander looked horrified at the very suggestion. Did he know of any students from that country? He did not.

It was the motoring magazine that led to the breakthrough.

Richard explained that he was not very keen an cars but was interested in aircraft.

"Oh, I am also, Sir Richard. My very rich Uncle Salem has one: it is a Piper. He has taken me up in it. He lives in Nairobi."

"Would you like to see mine. It is only a micro-light."

"Very much indeed. Sir Richard."

The red Thruster had not been flown since before the wedding. M.&B. Services, now under new management were told to get it ready and on the next Saturday morning the enthusiastic student was taken to Thelwell airfield. Mary's flying suit and head-set fitted him easily ... he was a slender young man ... and although it was a chilly late Autumn day the wind was light. Richard flew him round the circuit for twenty minutes or so and let him handle the controls and it was a very thrilled young man who allowed himself to be dragged away from the hangar to the club-room, where Henry the steward was serving cups of the vile brew he called coffee. It was not necessary to ask the lad whether he had enjoyed the experience: he was ecstatic. He was studying Economics, Law and Politics for his A Levels, and hoped to become a Barrister.

"Come and have lunch with us. I've told my wife to expect a guest."

Mary had earlier suggested that a vegetarian meal might be the safest option with an Indian visitor and they sat down to tinned Asparagus soup followed by Cauliflower Cheese. The boy had charming manners, was obviously intelligent and expressed himself clearly.

He was, he told them, fascinated by the introduction he was receiving into English Law: in this seventh week of the term he had begun the study of a branch of Law which had developed from a case in which an unfortunate plaintiff had swallowed the contents of a ginger beer bottle containing a decomposed snail. He went on to tell of several other equally revolting injuries caused by negligence. Even beginners in the Law are quite insensitive to the finer feelings.

Mary went to wash the dishes .... Mrs. Barlow would not come in on Saturdays ... and Richard took the opportunity to talk to the student alone.

"Iskander, do you mind if I ask you a question or two? Do you know why I am at the College?"

"Oh, we all know that, Sir Richard. You are a detective and it is because of the murder."

"Not a proper detective and it's not about the murder but something quite different. One of the members of the staff has disappeared ... some time before the murder ... and the Principal has asked me to investigate. Now there is a possibility that he may have gone to Africa and I thought, perhaps, that you could help me."

"That is most interesting. It is, of course Mr. Fordham of whom you are speaking. The students know all about it."

"I suppose they would. Now what I want to know is this: a number of students failed to re-appear after the summer vacation; and fourteen of them came from Africa. Could you get some information about them? I've got their names here ... find out if any of their friends are still in the College; their family background and so on, and, one very important point ... were any of them known for spending a good deal of money?"

"Not many students have much money."

"Naturally, I don't mean spending extravagantly; just more than one would expect."

"I will do that, Sir Richard: it will be most interesting."

"Good; but keep quiet about it. Don't even tell your girlfriend."

"I have no girlfriend. The English maidens are not friendly to Indians or Africans."

There seemed to be no answer to this sad statement but it was not so easy to persuade Iskander to leave. Mary returned and the young man poured out to her a long account of his family affairs, including the difficult matrimonial problems of his married sisters and the even greater troubles his father was having in finding suitable spouses for those still unmarried.

He left happily, in the end, promising to return with a report in a few days.

The College killing had ceased to be News. The funeral of Henry Seaforth was held at the local Methodist Church and Sir Richard contributed generously to the sending of a wreath by the General Studies Department. The house on the Larkhill Estate twice carried the notice UNDER OFFER and then reverted to FOR SALE. Mary met Miss Gartside at a Bring and Buy Sale in aid of Oxfam and was almost caught out when the former Headmistress asked after the health of her dear Aunt Jane. Christmas was approaching and the Bridgeminster Theatre Club had unwisely decided to do a pantomime. James Polk had been cast as Baron Hardup and found that with the rehearsals and the work involved in the Seaforth murder investigations he had few opportunities to drop in at India House.

Mary had not yet made an interesting announcement but was still working enthusiastically on the problem. Iskander did not return for a fortnight but when he did come it was with information.

He produced a chart and a map, made out neatly in coloured inks. Much work must have gone into them and the young man looked pleased with himself.

"The red stars, Sir Richard, show the places where the fourteen students lived. There are only nine because three lived in Capetown and four in Johannesburg. The lines on the map show the routes by which they travelled and which air-lines. Seven went home from London Airport, six from Gatwick and one from Stansted."

"How on earth did you find out all this? I'm very impressed."

"I have talked to their friends and told many lies."

"I know how it is ... go on."

"The chart I have made shows which of them spent most money. This boy bought a motor bike in his second term and also new clothes. This one was often at discotèques and had many girlfriends. I think those two spent the most, but all of these have had enough money, I think, except this one ... I call him Number 9."

"You're awfully good at charts, Iskander."

"We do many charts in Economics. I get very good marks for charts; always."

"You don't give their names."

"Is it necessary, Sir Richard? I would not like ..."

"I won't ask you now. You've been very helpful."

End of term was approaching. Richard' class was to end, as in the next session they were to be exposed to a course in Modern History. Richard invited the ten members to a small farewell party at India house: this surprised them; it is not the sort of thing that is done in Further Education, but they all turned up on the evening and all were quite respectably dressed: two even wore ties. Mary prepared sandwiches and little snacks and Richard concocted a Christmas Punch, the recipe for which he found in one of his wife's new cookery books. Prudently he reduced the quantity of Brandy specified: eighteen year olds are seldom able to judge their capacity and he had a nightmare vision of a headline: TEENAGERS DIE IN CRASH AFTER LECTURER'S PARTY. Seven of them came in two old cars.

After a sticky opening the party went quite well. Mary, her husband discovered, although only about seven years older than her guests, was treated almost as a mother figure: most of them were eager to confide in her and Richard had little to do except hand round food and pour out Punch in moderate helpings. One young fellow seemed an odd man out. Richard knew him as the only member of the class of science students who seemed to have an interest in Literature and during the last class of the term ... devoted to the Victorian poets ... had asked Richard if he believed that Tennyson and Arthur Hallam had had a homosexual relationship. To make conversation Richard asked him what he was studying and who were his teachers. He was in his second year of his A level course and had some hopes of getting to Cambridge to read Natural Sciences: his second choice was Imperial College, London. His name was Tony Bellenger.

His host had with difficulty scraped through O level Maths and the young man's description of the delights of Pure and Applied Mathematics meant nothing to him. The boy was an enthusiast and also had an admiration for the young lady teacher that had inspired him that went far beyond mere respect. In fact he was in love with her.

"She is so brilliant, Sir Richard. Not only is she a mathematician: she is also a linguist. There is Achmed in our class and she can talk to him in his own language."

"Where does this Achmed come from?"

"Somewhere in Africa, I am not sure ... no I remember it's called Tanzania." He went on in praise of the lady.

"You wouldn't think she was a teacher ... she is so good - looking and with such charm. She is not married."

He sighed audibly.

"I don't think I've met her. What is her name?"

"Miss Pienaar: Miss Trudi Pienaar," he sighed again.

"That is a Dutch name, I think."

"She told us that she was at the University of Capetown. They speak Dutch in South Africa, don't they?"

"Afrikaans: it's a sort of Dutch."

The ten students must have enjoyed the party for they were very reluctant to leave. Richard tried a discreet yawn or two at eleven o'clock which were ignored but it was his "What about a little music?" and the putting on a tape of The Mikado that finally shifted them. It was not their kind of music.

After the students had at last gone they sat in the Parlour and finished the last of the punch. Mary had again been doing her calculations but saw that Richard had become preoccupied: after all, tomorrow night would probably be just as suitable.

"You're very quiet," she said.

There was a long pause before he replied.

"You know, I think I've got it worked out. Not the murder, though I believe it's connected with the other thing. It was something that shy boy told me."

"I thought you were listening to him carefully. What did he say?"

"Enough to want me to put my theory to Jim Polk. There are things I want to know that only he can find out."

"Such as ...? I do hate you when you are being mysterious. Just like Holmes baffling Watson!"

"Come on, Watson; time for bed."

It was not too late after all.

Chapter 7

Jim Polk came next evening.

"Bosworth's made an arrest," were his first words.

Detective Sergeant Bosworth, newly promoted, had featured in two of Richard's cases and the Baronet bad no great faith in his abilities.

"Tell me all."

"Bosworth stopped a car on the by-pass ... rear light not working ..., and found three television sets in the back ... old lag named Parker; we've had a lot to do with him in the past. Searched his place and found ... well - first a lot of computers and word-processors, obviously nicked and also; guess what?"

"Well, from your manner I should think ... a gun."

Polk was disappointed.

"How do you make these guesses? Yes, it was a gun ... and what sort do you think?"

"Obviously a heavy-calibre revolver; a .45, probably."

Polk looked disgusted.

"Yes, it was, all nicely oiled and cleaned."

"Did he have any ammunition?"

"We didn't find it: probably kept it somewhere else."

"Could your forensic chaps tell if it had been fired recently?"

"They've got it now. I should get their report tomorrow."

Richard considered.

"But look, Jim; the `old lag' type of crook doesn't usually go in for using a gun, does he? Why should be have shot Seaforth?"

"Perhaps he got into the College looking for equipment to steal and the caretaker disturbed him. Don't forget Parker has a lot of convictions. He'd get a long sentence and he's not getting any younger."

"What have you charged him with?"

"Just possessing a fire-arm and stolen goods for the moment. We'll get it out of him, you'll see."

"What was his story about the gun."

"Usual load of cobblers. Said it was his father's who got it in Germany after the War. It's an American gun."

"It could be true."

Polk's tone did not bode well for the unlucky Parker.

"Has he got a Solicitor?"

"He'll get one on Legal Aid."

"No, tell him not to. I'll get my solicitors to see him. I want to have a chat with this Parker."

"I don't know what you're up to but you sound crafty. You kept me in the dark for a long time in that Thelwell case."

"Jim, I was going to ask you to come round and listen to my theory but this new happening alters things a bit. I think I know why Fordham disappeared and what he and some others were up to at the College. I know no more than you do about the murder ... but ... I'll bet you ... well, say a case of that Macallan whisky you like so much to ... what about a couple of front row seats for this pantomime you're in ... that the two are connected."

Polk was so moved that for the first time since Richard had known him he refused a drink and departed.

* * * * *

Next day Richard was greeted respectfully by the Senior Clerk (now called a Legal Executive) at Marples the Solicitors. Marples is one of the oldest established firms in the South of England, and unusually there are still Marples family members. 'Old Mr. Marples', now in his seventies is semi-retired: 'Young Mr. Marples' at fifty, looks after the small amount of criminal work that the firm undertakes. Richard had not met him when visiting the office in connection with the conveyancing of India House or his marriage settlement.

"Rather unusual, Sir Richard, but I suppose you have a reason for paying for the man's defence. Of course I know him: before the Crown Prosecution Service took over I prosecuted him once or twice for the Police. `Andrew Parker' was it; no, Arthur Parker, that's the man. Just a small time burglar: he'll know me."

"I'm fairly certain that he had nothing to do with this murder. Polk hasn't charged him yet with anything but he very likely will. I'd very much like to talk to the man. He's still at the Police Station: could you get me in as your clerk, or something like that."

"The Police won't mind. I get on well with Jim Polk: would this afternoon be suitable?"

A uniformed Constable led Richard and the solicitor to a gloomy interview room in the basement of the Bridgeminster Police Station. Parker was already seated at a small table and his visitors took the two vacant seats.

The Constable remained outside.

"This is Sir Richard Smith, Parker. He is offering to pay for your defence ... if you are willing to answer some questions."

The Victorian criminologist, Lombroso used to publish photographs of 'criminal types' and his theories had a certain vogue in the nineties. Arthur Parker had a visage that combined all of them. His face showed cunning, avarice, fear and plain cheek.

"I've heard of you. Sort of amateur `tec aren't you and a millionaire. You'll have to pay for me to answer questions."

"Don't be a fool, Parker. The Police have got you cold on the fire-arms charge. There's a big panic on about guns and you could get the maximum ... with your record."

"That gun's never been fired in my lifetime, Mr. Marples. My Dad brought it back from the War. I never had no bullets for it neither."

"It's gone for forensic testing, remember."

"Yes, and what's to stop some of them cops firing a few rounds in it to frame me? Just like they did with that knife they pinned on Sammy Connolly?"

"Sammy knew all about knives."

"Yes, he did, I grant you. But he swore to me in the Scrubs that he never touched that one."

Arthur Parker had a good line in outraged innocence.

"Look, Mr. Parker", Richard put in, "if the gun was just a relic why was it kept oiled and cleaned?"

"Why not for the kiddies to play with?"

"Come on Arthur, you can do better than that: you've never had any kids, have you?"

Young Mr. Marples knew how to deal with petty crooks like Parker.

The burglar paused to think.

"O.K. Mr. Marples, I'll come clean with you. You're my lawyer ain't you and you can't say nothing about what I tell you? One of my friends ... never mind who ... told me that there's people up in London who'll pay well to hire out a gun ... particularly one that's never been used. I thought I might make a bit out of it. It was my Dad's."

"So you oiled it and kept it by you?" Richard put in.

"Right, Guv'nor: but I never did find anyone who wanted it."

"Do you know anyone who might have done a job at the College, Arthur. You specialise in electrical stuff, don't you?'

"Now you know I'm not one to grass, Mr. Marples: never have and never will."

"Ever thought of doing a job there yourself?"

"Well, I'll be honest with you: I have looked round the place. Do you know, anyone can walk in and out of there and nobody checks anyway. A lot of the stuff is out of date and all with code marks on."

There seemed to be no more information to be got out of Arthur Parker.

"I'll come and see you again in a few days, Parker," Marples said. "I expect they'll move you to Portborough jail tomorrow. We'll get a good man for your defence."

"Better than that young Humphrey chap I had last time on Legal Aid. Stammered and stuttered like a kid who didn't know his lessons. Could have done better myself."

They stood up to go but Parker had one more thing to say.

"I 'eard about you, Sir Richard. You was up at Foxwood wasn't you, after all them break-ins. One of my mates said ..."

"I shouldn't talk about that if I was you, Mr. Parker. You might get into more trouble."

Young Mr. Marples had not heard about the Foxwood case and looked extremely puzzled.

"What about another weekend break?" Richard asked Mary over breakfast.

"I know you," was her reply. "I saw the way you looked at your breakfast. You're thinking of those `Full English Breakfasts' you got at that Hotel."

Her husband had indeed looked at his bowl of Muesli without enthusiasm; Mary was still keen on getting his weight down. Unknown to him she had also obtained another pamphlet ... 'The Ideal Diet for the Pregnant Woman' which promised even greater austerities.

"We could go to Bristol and you could take your cousins their Christmas presents."

"Could we go by train? The weather's so awful for driving." A wet, cold winter was beginning.

"Right, and I think I can afford to go First Class. I'll go to the travel agents and get details of hotels."

"No need: there's an A.A. book in the car."

"Well, I want to see some travel agents, actually."

"You've got an idea, haven't you?"

"Yes; I'll tell you about it this evening."

There are four travel agents in Bridgeminster, one an independent concern and the others branches of National companies. A fifth had gone bankrupt about a year ago, leaving several hundred citizens to face holidays at home. The firm's low prices had been achieved by its failure to join a professional client insurance scheme.

Richard had worked out a plan. It was crude and required the telling of a great many untruths: it was only partially successful.

"One of my colleagues at the College told me that you made his travel arrangements for him."

"Who was that, Sir Richard?"

"Mr. Tredwin, actually."

"We used to do his bookings for trips to Russia and Bulgaria: we haven't done anything for him recently."

"I think Mr. ... now what was his name ... he comes to you."

"Was it Mr. Mortimer? He's at the College. What can we do for you Sir Richard?"

Richard feigned interest in Safaris in Kenya, Sailing Holidays in Greek waters and Pony Trekking in the Welsh mountains and left with a bundle of pamphlets.

At the next two agents he mentioned the names of several other College lecturers but there was no response. At the fourth a poster showing the bulb fields of Holland with wind-mills in the background, caught his eye. It offered coach tours of that country next Spring. It gave him an idea.

The girl behind the counter wearing a uniform rather like that of an Air Hostess was most helpful.

"I am thinking of taking my car to Holland next Spring and I wondered if you could give me the brochures and time-tables for the ferries. The shortest sea crossing ... my wife suffers terribly from seasickness."

This was a gross slander: it was Richard who often felt queasy in a Force 5 blow.

"Here you are Sir; Dover Zeebrugge, Felixstowe-Hook of Holland, Dover-Ostend; they are all here."

"I think one of the teachers at the College told me that she goes frequently to Holland ... I do some teaching there, you know. What was it I was told? One of the routes has very large ships ... very comfortable and stable."

"Oh, yes: that will be Miss Pienaar: she goes quite often. I think she has some relations living there and pops over frequently. She was joking last time that she ought to have a season ticket."

"Of course, I remember now, it was she that told me. A charming young lady ... drives a white Mini, I think."

The girl looked puzzled.

"No, I don't think so. This is the only travel agency in Bridgeminster where you can park outside so I would remember. She used to have a red sports car; very smart and before that a blue one."

"Oh well, she certainly told me that you arranged her tickets very efficiently. I'll come in again when we've decided the dates."

The Lecturers at Bridgeminster College are provided with stickers to place on the windscreens of their cars to gain admission to the Staff car park. It was unfortunate that the batch provided that year had poor powers of adhesion and Richard's like many others had fallen off. The attendant, who lived in a little wooden hut at the entrance nevertheless waved him through with a friendly smile. Leaving his car, he walked back to the hut as if to pass the time of day.

"Not too bad a day for December, Leslie."

"We've had enough of that old rain, Sir Richard. Students have had their game cancelled for this afternoon; pitch flooded."

"I ought to get a new sticker for my windscreen. They are talking about giving me another class for next term. You recognised my car: do you know all the Staff Cars?"

"Pretty well, I reckon. Some of them keep changing their vehicles, particularly the chaps that teach Motor Engineering. I think they buy them; do them up and make a bit out of it."

Richard hesitated and then put the question.

"Tell me, Les, are there any others who change their cars frequently?"

The gate-keeper was no fool: he had sensed that Richard's tone had changed and for a moment became wary.

"Why would you want to know that, I wonder", he said.

Fortunately at that point a pair of students in a battered Fiesta tried to drive into the Staff Car Park to be repelled by an indignant Les. By the time he returned Richard had decided.

"Did you know that I was asked by the Principal to investigate ..."

"The murder?"

"No, quite a different matter: it's confidential and I can't tell you much about it now but it would be a great help ..."

"I've heard about your detective work. My brother Cyril is in the Police. You want to know about cars?"

"About people changing their cars."

"It's mostly the younger teachers. They buy what they think are marvellous bargains and then they have trouble with them. Women keep their cars generally. That Miss

Osborne, she's got a Beetle she bought new in 1972. Mind you there's a glamorous blonde in Science Department ... I don't know her name ... the students all fall for her ... she must have plenty of money 'cos she has a new car every six months. She's got a Mini now, but she won't keep it long. Now if it was motor bikes you wanted to know about there's one of the Lab Technicians: he's had more machines written off than I can remember ... rides like a maniac."

"Thanks, Les, that's very helpful. Don't tell anyone I've been asking questions."

Leaving the parking attendant Richard walked round the vast car park examining the rows of cars. There were fifty-two Minis, four of them white, three of them old and rusty, the fourth almost new. Its G.B. plate showed that it had been transported by European Ferries.

That evening Richard set out his solution of the College Mystery to Mary. It took him almost an hour, to give her his theory that explained the disappearance of Edward Fordham and the murder of Henry Seaforth.

"It's a nice story you've thought up," was her comment. "It explains what they were up to and it makes sense ... but was what they were doing against the law ...?"

"I don't know, but murder is, and there must be a connection."

"There's one thing you haven't explained."

"What's that?"

"The letter sent to the Principal. What was the reason for it?"

"I don't know: I lay awake last night thinking about it."

"I don't believe it. You always fall asleep straightaway ... afterwards!"

"Nonsense! But you're quite right: it's not so much who sent that letter as why. It didn't say anything definite; just `up to something'."

"Jim Polk is bound to ask. I suppose you're going to tell him what you've just told me."

"Very soon; I thought of asking him to come round yesterday but I changed my mind. You've given me an idea, though. I'll go round to the Station tomorrow morning and see him."

More than a year after Sir Richard's first case the men of Bridgeminster Police Station were now familiar with the City's amateur investigator.

The desk sergeant, passed him through and he found James Polk in his small office studying a list of stolen goods recently recovered from a local 'fence'.

"Found your lost sheep, then?" he asked.

"Very nearly, Jim, or at least, I hope so. What I wanted was to have another look at that bit of paper ... the one with the message Dr. Floodgate got."

"I told you; there were no prints an it."

"I know; can you find it?"

Polk took an envelope from the drawer of his desk and handed over the slip of paper. It was about six inches by three, but Richard, borrowing Polk's ruler measured it carefully and wrote down the exact measurements.

"Now look at this carefully, Jim. Three of the edges are accurately cut by the machine that produced it. The top edge seems to have been cut with a scissors; it's not perfectly straight."

"So what?"

"If this was torn off a memo pad or something of the sort there might have been words printed at the top."

"You mean like this one?"

Polk produced a pad in which each sheet was headed 'Bridgeminster Police Station'.

"Yes, just like that: in this case I suggest that the heading was `Bridgeminster College of Advanced Education'."

"Very likely from what you've told me."

"Let me have that slip: I'm going round to the College to ask a few questions."

It was the last week of term and the car parks were less full than usual. The lecturers were all present but many students were in the habit of extending their Christmas vacations. In the Department of General Studies he asked to see its head. Mr. Gillette, known to his staff as 'Cutthroat', was an amiable man who had been desk-bound for so long that he had no idea of the problems involved in teaching the youth of the nineties. He had written to Richard asking him to take another class in the next term: would he be willing to take over an evening class in Modern Literature from a teacher who had been taken ill?

Richard's first thought had been, 'How modern?' For him poetry had died before T.S. Eliot and the English novel with Thomas Hardy (although he liked Evelyn Waugh) and the thought of having to read up Isherwood, Auden ... and worst of all, Dylan Thomas, in the interest of criminal investigation, was painful. However he listened earnestly to Mr. Gillette as he explained the syllabus half completed by the unfortunate teacher.

"I'm afraid the course is only Grade 3 ... £10 an hour; do you mind?"

"Richard did not mind; he was looking at the corner of Mr. Gillette's desk.

"Do you mind if I jot down a few notes. I haven't got my diary with me. May I have a sheet from your pad?"

Gillette tore one off and passed it across the table. It carried the heading 'Bridgeminster College of Technology'.

Richard scribbled rapidly on the sheet remarking as he put it away.

"A bit out of date, are you not? I thought it is now the College of Advanced Education."

"Oh, we're using up old stock. The Administrative Wing has been given the new stationary."

There seemed to be no way of avoiding the class in very modern literature and Richard took his leave. Outside in the corridor he compared the sheet of paper he had been given with that which had carried the obscure message. It was a few millimetres wider.

In the Administration Wing he asked to see Miss Penfold. He was kept waiting for some time in the outer office where a number of clerks sat looking into computer screens: the chair was most uncomfortable. When he was called into the Registrar's office her manner was chilly.

"Really, Sir Richard, you must know that I am a very busy person. The end of term is a particularly trying period. I have given you access to all the documents you have asked to see."

"I am very sorry to have to trouble you again. If the matter was not so serious ..."

"Serious? Edward Fordham had a perfect right to go off if he wished. I don't know why there is all this fuss."

"Are you sure you don't know? Have you seen this before?"

Richard took from his pocket the slip of paper with the message printed in ball-point.

"'He was up to something', it says. Did you know what he was up to. Do you have a memo-pad of this size ... the new stock, I understand?"

"I have nothing to say, I shall consult the Principal."

"This was sent to Dr. Floodgate: I wonder why."

"He has a right to know about everything that goes on in the College. He has a most difficult task and many of the Lecturers do not give him full support. I hate disloyalty."

A more emotional tone had crept into the formerly chilly Miss Penfold's voice.

"You have a warm regard for Dr. Floodgate?" Richard gave the word `warm' the smallest possible emphasis but the Assistant Registrar recognised it. She showed some little confusion for a moment and was silent. Eventually she spoke.

"I really have nothing more to say, Sir Richard. I have done nothing wrong."

Before returning home he visited the welding shop. Graham Parsons was demonstrating the use of a dangerous looking oxyacetylene burner to a group of students; some of them seemed inattentive and the visitor reflected that failing to grasp the method correctly might result in serious accidents.

"All right, lads, that's enough for today."

Parsons extinguished the torch and removed his goggles.

"Richard Smith: what can I do for you? Want some new gates for the back entrance. I'd love to do a matching set but it would cost you a pretty penny."

"One day, Graham, I promise you. No, what I wanted to ask you was about that day when you thought someone had been doing some welding at the weekend. You said you detected a smell of paint. What sort of paint?"

Graham Parsons reflected for a moment.

"It's a while back but I think it was cellulose. We might put a coat of rust proofing paint on a job in here but that was a different smell."

"Like they use on cars?"

"Yes, probably."

"There weren't any traces of paint? On the floor, for instance?"

"Sorry, I didn't look."

"Do you mind if I do?"

Richard crossed the workshop towards the double doors and carefully examined the concrete floor. There were one or two traces of paint of different colours but he realised that it would need an expert to learn anything from them.

"Come around one evening for a drink, Graham, and I'll show you where those gates will go."

This was not a ploy; the owner of India House had already decided to replace the ugly pair that gave access to what had once been a small stable yard.

At lunch Richard reported the results of the morning's work.

"She virtually admitted that she wrote that note but the question is how did she know that Fordham was going to do a bunk?"

"Why did she send it?"

"I think she's in love with Floodgate ... one of these frustrated spinsters."

"Don't be unkind. I was a frustrated spinster until ... let me see ... ten and a half weeks ago."

"But seriously, the letter shows that she must have got wind of the game that was going on ... how?"

"Did you ask her?"

"No; useless: she pretty tough. Polk might get it out of her, though. By the way, where's your brother at the moment."

"John? He's at Portsmouth while his ship refits. He rang the other day when you were out. He's living ashore and I've got a 'phone number. Why do you want to know?"

"Something I want to ask him about guns. He's a gunnery officer, isn't he?"

"He says it's all missiles now and they don't give the same satisfaction."

Richard rather wondered how one could get satisfaction from either guns or missiles, but that evening he got through to John Hutchins.

"Hello, John, Richard here. I hope we've written to thank you for your splendid wedding present."

Richard had actually forgotten what the Lieutenant's present was.

"Oh, rather; Mary wrote: I don't think husbands ever do write."

The two men chatted for some minutes. John Hutchins wanted to know the name and address of one of the bridesmaids.

"The dark one ... we got talking after you and Mary left and I promised to look her up ... nice girl, but I forget her name."

"I'll get Mary to find out; they're friends. Look, John, you know all about guns don't you?"

"Richard, when you've passed the Navy's course, all you don't know about guns could be written on a postcard. Mind you, we don't have any big guns in the Navy now. What do you want to know?"

"Revolvers."

"Ah, yes; I read about the Bridgeminster Murder. I hope it won't spoil my promotion prospects having a brother-in-law mixed up in unsavoury criminal cases. Some of these Admirals still think we're officers and Gentlemen."

"If they sack you I'll have to buy you a small battle-ship to play with. Can you tell me what sort of revolver is called Heavy Calibre?"

".45 or .38, both powerful weapons."

"Are they very heavy?"

"Pretty solid and they have a real kick. I've fired them on a range."

"Could a woman use one?"

"Not Mary ... she hasn't got the wrists: or that dainty little bridesmaid: I've just remembered her name was Emma. You won't forget to ask Mary for her 'phone number?"

"So a woman could use a heavy revolver?"

"Oh yes. Don't forget one doesn't handle them today like John Wayne in the old movies. You hold the gun in your right hand and rest it on your left forearm. More accurate that way, though hand guns are not really much use except at very short range. All that stuff about drilling the Ace of Spades at fifty yards is rubbish."

"Thanks very much, John. Would you like to speak to Mary?"

"I'd better ask her if you've stopped beating her yet."

Mary took over the 'phone and the handsome young officer was given the address of the more glamorous of her two bridesmaids.

"She's a very nice girl and a much better housekeeper than I am," Mary told her husband later. "When her mother went off with a man she had to look after her little brother and sister. I wouldn't want John to marry a flighty girl."

When young women have solved their own matrimonial problems they are apt to develop match-making tendencies!

Chapter 8

They invited James Polk to come round but he pleaded the penultimate rehearsal of 'Cinderella' so the following day was agreed on.

"Come early, Jim, and don't bother to have a meal first; Mary will get us something to eat. What about six o'clock?"

Inspector Polk never refused an invitation to eat out; his grumpy wife ... and she had a lot to be grumpy about ... had long ago given up any serious culinary efforts. It was a cold night and in the Georgian fire-place of the Parlour pine logs burned cheerfully. Mary had put up Christmas decorations, remarking wistfully as she put a tinsel Angel on the top of the tree: "It's really a festival for children, isn't it?"

Polk arrived promptly and was placed in an easy chair before the fire with a table at his elbow carrying his usual refreshment and a plate of interesting looking canapés that had been the former head chef's subject at the last cookery class of the term. Polk had brought his large Christmas Card with him ... a revolting, bright coloured study of robins in the snow, which Mary tactfully placed in the centre of the mantel piece beneath Uncle Malcolm's portrait. They had moved the fast-food king from the dining-room; the pork pie looked wrong there. They sat and made small talk for some minutes and Polk made the first contribution to the subject that was in all their minds.

"Before you tell me anything I'd better tell you that there was nothing to show that the gun Parker had was the one. They are ninety-nine per cent certain that it hadn't been fired for ages; they've got pretty good methods at Forensic. Nice, these little snacks ... where did you get them?"

Mary looked pleased.

"I made them: I've got some more in the kitchen but don't eat too many; I've got supper for later."

Richard re-filled Polk's glass and poured sherry for himself and Mary.

"I never thought that Parker had used that gun," Richard observed, "I was even rather surprised that he thought of hiring it out. His type does not aspire to violent crime ... or so I've read in books. You would know better than I."

"Granted, but he's a nasty bit of work. We're still holding him, by the way; plenty of charges possible. Well, let's have this theory of yours."

Richard opened the folder that lay by his chair and took out a sheaf of notes.

"I don't suppose you brought a note-book, Jim, but it doesn't matter. I've made a copy of all my notes for you. Now, listen carefully; I shall say this only once."

"I'll deal first with the disappearance of Edward Fordham. You put the Principal on to me and he came round on the day after the wedding, when, I must say, we weren't particularly keen on having visitors."

Mary blushed.

"Now the first thing that occurred to me was that the appointment of a top City man to a job in a provincial college was a very unusual one. I went to see my stock-broker in London and he gave me the man's background. He was earning many times his Bridgeminster salary when he was in business. Furthermore, if he had wanted a change he could have joined his brother's firm; which is a large industrial concern in the Midlands.

"The brother is one Charles Fordham, Managing Director with a controlling share in the Company. I'll come back to him later."

"There was another clue that indicated that Edward Fordham never intended to make a career in Bridgeminster ... the house on the Larkhill estate. It's a very small place for a man on even the salary earned by a college head of department ... I've visited one of the ordinary lecturers who had a much more impressive place ... and also it had ... well, what I would describe as a temporary look: a camp rather than a home. Missing the woman's touch, too."

"He had a wife, though?"

"We'll suppose so. The neighbour, who is a nosey old lady saw her very seldom and said she was away often, describing her as having reddish hair. She also said that she was much younger than Fordham."

Jim Polk bit into another canapé.

"Nothing to go on yet," he observed with his mouth full.

"Now we come to Africa."

"Cor, why not Weston-super-Mare?" Polk, influenced by the whisky, the selection of tasty morsels and the warm fire was becoming more jocular.

"Africa keeps coming into it. When I visited the Fordham house with Cringle, the house-agent, there was a letter on the doormat with a bright yellow stamp. I couldn't read the name of the country but I discovered that there are only three countries issuing similar stamps at the present time. One is an African Republic which is at present in the final stages of a bloody Civil War."

"I read about it in the paper ... Thousands massacred."

"It's called Gambonia ... keep it in mind. Africa comes into the case again. When I went round the house with Mr. Cringle there was a bookcase containing a few dozen volumes: half were books about golf and the rest travel books, chiefly on Africa. Now, when I re-visited the house the Africa books were gone. I suspect that someone realised that they might have put ideas into a visitor's head and quietly removed them. I think I know who."

Polk glanced at his glass in a meaningful manner.

"Pour him a small one, Mary; he's got to keep his head clear until I've finished. She knows how to pour small ones, Jim!"

"Now there's another indication. The College has quite a number of African students and same failed to return in September to finish their two year courses."

"Wouldn't there often be drop-outs?"

"There would, but not as many as fourteen. Remember, too, that they came from countries fairly near to Gambonia ... and ... although I haven't been able to check them all, it seems that some, at least, were by student standards, big spenders."

"Bringing in drugs ... very common."

"Not drugs, I think, but bringing in something."

"What?"

"Wait a moment. This Gambonia has been having a Civil War for a long time but about three years ago the rebel forces began to get hold of large supplies of weapons. Fordham has been at the College for rather longer than that."

"I don't see the connection."

"Wait a bit. Suppose, Jim, that you wanted to organise a criminal enterprise that needed, say, a financial expert, somebody fluent in several languages, a person with a thorough knowledge of precious stones ... and a good welder. Where would you go to recruit them?"

"The Scrubs, Parkhurst, Ford Prison,"

"True, but you'd have to wait a while for their services. Dr. Floodgate said that you could find almost any skill on his staff ... he was quite proud of it."

"O.K., I see that, but you haven't told me what the game was."

Here Mary intervened. "Shall we go to the dining-room and have supper. You can go on telling Jim while we eat."

"You make a wonderful soup, Mary," was Polk's comment as he took his first spoonful.

"Sorry, it's Baxter's Royal Game with a dash of Port added. I didn't have time to make home-made with the Christmas presents to pack. I did the next course, though."

It was salmon with a Hollandaise sauce that the new housewife had been taught to make to a professional standard at the College and it was not until it had been sufficiently praised that the guest showed a willingness to hear more.

"You were saying that the College was the place to sign up a safe-busting gang."

"Not safe-busting ... a more profitable activity. Now just suppose, Jim, that you're leading a band of Freedom Fighters ... or a gang of terrorists, whichever way you look at it ... in the African jungle, and all you've got is a few worn-out Kalashnikovs. What do you want most?"

"More guns, bombs and things."

"Right, but you've got a problem."

"No problem: the world's awash with surplus weapons left over from the Cold War."

"But you need money to buy them and someone clever to organise the supply. Remember lots of countries have banned the export of arms. There's a lot of money in supplying weapons. Remember that Parker was hoping to make big money hiring out an old gun."

"The little rat: I'm going to throw the book at him!"

"Quite right: but remember this, Gambonia is one of the poorest countries in the world. The Soviets used to pour money and weapons into countries like that, but fortunately they've got a better use for their money now."

"So?"

"I'm coming to it." Richard re-filled Polk's glass with an excellent dry white wine they had found in the Loire Valley and with which they had almost overloaded the car. Mary offered him cheese and biscuits and her husband went on.

"Gambonia is a poor country but some years ago a survey showed that it had potential for the discovery of minerals. Long ago gold was mined there."

"You think they found a gold mine?"

"No, not gold. Mary here is not just beautiful: she's also intellectually brilliant" ... it is always easier to praise your wife when you have had a glass or two of wine ... "she got a Grade A in Geography. I got out one of her old text-books and found that in the Western region of Gambonia ... the region, by the way, where the rebellion began ... there are extinct volcanoes."

"What can they do with those?"

"Have you heard of Kimberley?"

"I did O level Geography and just scraped through. It's in South Africa."

"Right, and Diamonds are found in the pipes of old volcanoes, usually in a sort of blue mud."

"Ah, yes, I begin to see."

"If these rebels have got a supply of diamonds what do they need? Someone to market them ... and it would have to be done very discreetly to avoid swamping the market and they need someone who knows the different qualities of the stones and they have to get them transported to Europe. With all that organised they've got the money to buy any amount of guns, missiles ... anything you like to name. And remember this, Edward Fordham's brother is the big boss of B.L.W. Ltd."

"And what's that?"

"Birmingham Light Weapons: they make everything from pistols to light artillery."

"So the game was exporting weapons illegally?"

"Exactly: that involved bringing in uncut diamonds ... they would look like rough pebbles I suppose ... getting them sold and turning the proceeds into guns. Then it was the brother who runs B.L.W.'s job."

"So you reckon they got students from Africa to bring them in? Eventually one would talk."

"Well would he? What would he know?"

"They would have to tell each student what they were up to."

"Would they? I can think of half a dozen stories to cover it."

"I can't."

"What about this one ...

"'Hello, Achmed, I hear you're going home for the holidays. Lucky you, it'll be Summer there won't it? Look, could you do me a favour? There's a shop in Mandela Street in Jo'burg .. name of Patel ... where my wife bought some lovely native jewellery when she was visiting her South African cousins last year. Tell the man that you want a piece like the one Mrs. Bloggs bought last year ... he'll remember.' How's that: want another?"

"You've got a criminal mind."

"It's reading English Literature. Start with Dickens, Jim ... no, better still, Trollope; Dickens relies too much on coincidence. Have you ever thought what were the odds against Steerforth's body being washed up on the beach where little Emily had lived?"

Jim Polk thought it all out and Mary helped him to an exciting looking iced pudding. On their honeymoon they had acquired the French habit of eating the dessert after the cheese.

"Wait a moment," he said, "didn't you tell me that some of these young chaps had been given money?"

"Do you want another story to explain how that was covered? `Buy the things for me Abdul ... I think the price was £200: here's the money and if you can get it for less, keep the balance for yourself. It'll help with your holiday expenses. That shop keeper looked as if he would haggle.' Of course he would haggle and the boy would go away happy! Want another story?"

"The Mafia ought to send their kids to that Oxford College of yours: perhaps they do ... It's far-fetched but it might fit."

Polk had finished his pudding but accepted a second helping.

He had been thinking.

"When you gave me a list of skills needed you said `knowing foreign languages' and ... what was it ... `knowledge of precious stones'."

"Have you ever thought, Jim, that if you're trying to talk to someone in, say, French, it's not so difficult to pass the time of day or to do some simple shopping, but a problem if you want to give detailed instructions, particularly of a technical nature."

"Don't I know it: last time I was in France and the clutch went two miles out of Le Havre it was a nightmare. Do you know the French for `clutch'?"

"No. Now these students had to be given exact instructions as to what they had to do. There are people in that College who speak many languages. There's an ex-Baptist minister turned Atheist who speaks Chinese. Now here the gang had a lot of luck."

"How so?"

"There is one Lecturer who speaks a number of languages fluently, including at least one African tongue, probably Swahili; it is used in East Africa. The countries round Gambonia were once colonies of Portugal and

France so I expect those languages would be useful. The person in question also speaks Afrikaans."

"Cape Dutch?"

"Right: now by a lucky chance that person is also a graduate in Crystallography."

"And what exactly is that?"

"Diamonds are crystals."

"Ah," Polk became sunk in thought.

"Shall we have our coffee in The Parlour," Mary asked. "I'll allow you a liqueur with it as it's almost Christmas."

They passed from the dining-room to the fireside chairs beneath Uncle Malcolm's stern gaze and Richard poured three glasses of Cointreau. It was a mark of Polk's concentration on the problem that he accepted his: normally he rejected 'fancy drinks' and stuck to whisky.

"I'd better send Bosworth up to Hatton Garden, tomorrow. Somebody there can be got to talk."

"Not there ... Amsterdam, and the street is "Niewe Uilenburgerstraat. I rang the Commercial Attaché at the Dutch Embassy. Most of the diamond merchants are found there.

"Why?"

"It's a world centre for diamond cutting and the person I mentioned has been going there regularly, and, of course, speaks Dutch. I opened the drinks cupboard and there was a bottle of Dutch Schnapps ... half full. I've never tried it; have you?"

"Foul stuff! This Contreau isn't bad, though."

"Can we have another, Mary?"

"Yes, but I'll pour them." She did!

They finished their coffee, Jim Polk looking rather dissatisfied.

"Well", he said, "you've probably done it again. A nice bit of Smith guess-work and we'll have to pull this

Fordham chap in. It's not particularly wicked though, is it? More like that `guns for Iraq business ... political: I thought you would tell me that you'd got it all tied up with the College murder."

"Oh, but I have."

Polk had no words to utter, and Richard glanced at his notes.

"You've forgotten that there was one other skill that I mentioned ... welding. Graham Parsons, the Senior Lecturer in that subject ... I forgot to tell you, Mary, he's going to make us some proper gates for the stable yard ... he told me on the Monday after the murder that he found evidence that someone had been using the welding equipment in the workshop between about 3 p.m. on the Sunday and the Monday morning. Also, there was a smell of paint ... cellulose paint."

"Was he working there on the Sunday?"

"Yes, a private job; slightly irregular. Now Seaforth, the chief caretaker, went away with his wife most Saturday evenings and came back early on Monday morning, leaving his deputy in charge. If anyone wanted to use that equipment secretly the best opportunity would be when Seaforth was away. He would know because the caretaker has no garage and his car is always parked by his bungalow: no car; no caretaker. His deputy lives two miles away."

"Then why did they pick a night when he was at home?"

"His car was in for repairs and his wife was away. She says he was an early-to-bed man. They would think his house empty."

"But who are `they'?"

"Now I'm really going to do some guesswork. Tell me, Jim, what's the really safe way to hide something in a car?"

"I've heard of some very clever dodges from the Customs chaps at Portborough ... oh. I get it ... welding."

"A very small amount needed. Just a bit of thin metal welded to the chassis and covering a million pounds worth of diamonds; a touch of paint from one of those canister things you can buy to cover up scratches on the wings of the car and you're pretty safe from any Customs check. You won't use the same car more than once or twice so you're probably the sort of person who changes your car frequently. I forgot to tell you, the welding shop has double doors wide enough to admit a small vehicle. Holland's not so far that someone with family connections there might not make frequent short visits. Another thing, Jim, I suspect that this was the last consignment."

"Why?"

"The Gambonian rebels are on the point of taking the capital. They'll be the legal government soon and won't need to smuggle diamonds out. B.S.W. Ltd. will be able to sell them guns openly."

"I ask again: why was Seaforth shot?"

"My guess is this. Somebody was doing the welding in that shop when the caretaker did a late night check-up. The man probably gave some sort of explanation which might, or might not have satisfied ... but ..."

"Wait a moment; who was the man?"

"He could have been one of several members of the engineering department; Graham Parsons told me that most of them could do a bit of welding, but, on the whole I think it was Ted Morgan."

"Who is he?"

"The assistant lecturer in welding. I was twice in that workshop and each time there was a man in there who did not seem keen to make my acquaintance."

"So he shot Seaforth?"

"No: he wouldn't have a gun at the College and I don't suppose he's the type to use one. He plays only a small part in the game. He was working on the car, hiding the gems ... a white Mini, I think and when he finished the job he drove it to its owner. He told her that he'd been disturbed ..."

"Wait a moment ... her?"

"Yes, a young lady that you're going to want to meet ... I haven't met her myself though I think I've seen her across the staff room; a person who speaks all the languages, knows all about precious stones, and ... drives a white Mini. Incidentally she has changed her car frequently in the last year or so and comes from South Africa where, I'm told, they carry guns like we carry umbrellas."

"What's her name?"

"Trudi Pienaar, or at least that's the name she goes under. I've been wondering, though, whether she isn't really Trudi Fordham. I went through the staff records carefully. The lady is given as living in a flat in the City, actually in a block next to the one where I lived before entering into wedded bliss ..."

"Cut all that out, Richard, and get on with it."

"Miss Gartside told me that there were two women seen at number twenty, the wife and a visitor who she thought might be a relative as there was a similarity. The hair colour was different ... did you know Jim that women sometimes use wigs? The witness also says that one of the two wore a hat: useful things hats. I'm suggesting that Miss Pienaar and the visitor were one and the same person: sometimes she spent periods living with Fordham as his wife and sometimes at her flat. She is the person who has been going to the house since the disappearance of Fordham. It's obvious that they didn't want the house sold immediately. The asking price was absurd and several offers were rejected."

"... Of course they may not actually be married. There's a lot of that sort of thing going on today ... it's a permissive age and when I think what I had to pay for the choir, organist and Church fees I ..."

"You got a bargain," Mary put in. "Cut out the heavy Victorian jokes, it makes you sound middle-aged. Tell Jim the rest."

"Not much more to tell. We can only guess where Fordham's gone or why the woman didn't go too. Cringle has been told to send on letters but he was probably given only a forwarding address. You might try `Post Restante', Birmingham. Don't forget, when you find him he's going to look a bit different. He asked Phil Pyle about hair dyes."

"Why Birmingham: oh, I see, the brother. Where's the woman, though?"

"I expect you'll find her. She must be the killer of Seaforth. When she heard that the welding job had been disturbed she would have driven to somewhere near the College ... got in ... they are very careless about keys, I'm told and she must have got hold of one ... and found the poor chap doing his rounds. Cold-blooded."

"She could have got away already."

"I saw her in the College a few days ago ... I wonder, though ... let's find out. It's only nine o'clock and the old lady won't have gone to bed yet."

There are four telephone extensions in India House and Richard went to the one in the corner of the room and dialled a number.

"Miss Gartside? I hope I am not disturbing you at this late hour but do you remember that when you gave us that delightful tea some time ago you mentioned that you had been suffering from interference with your television set. Now I was talking to an expert who teaches at the College and he suggested a remedy."

"Cor - he does think up a quick yarn, your husband," Polk muttered sotto voce."

"Oh, Sir Richard, how kind of you! Do you know it's been very bad the last two days. I thought it was something Mr. Fordham had working but it can't have been because the house is empty. I couldn't watch the repeat of `Porridge' this evening: I do love Ronnie Barker, don't you?"

"I'll get my friend to look at your set."

"You are so kind, Sir Richard. Do give my regards to Lady Smith: you have such a charming wife."

Richard put down the 'phone, scribbling a note on a pad to remind himself of another deception.

"What's all this about television, then?" Polk asked.

"She's there, Jim. I didn't tell you about the interference. I believe they had a radio transmitter going in that house, probably hidden in the loft. I noticed when I was last there that the mains power was still on; unwise if a house is empty. That's how they kept in touch ... Gambonia, Holland, Birmingham and probably other places. Safer than telephones. We know she's been visiting the place and the house has very heavy curtains: no-one would notice if there were lights on.

Polk stood up, a picture of indecision.

"I suppose I'll have to go down to the Station and contact the Superintendent. I came round on foot because ..."

They both knew the reason.

"... can you lend me your car?"

"I'll ring for a taxi ... on Police expenses, mind. May I come with you?"

Polk hesitated. "If it's .Chief Inspector Morris it'll be all right but the Super doesn't like amateurs. Still, you've been a real help this time ... I'll ask."

Swiftsure Taxis is an efficient firm. Within five minutes a cab arrived and they were driven to the Police Station.

From his office Polk made a number of 'phone calls and both Superintendent Garrett and Inspector Morris arrived within half an hour. Sergeant Bosworth took longer to contact, but eventually the intelligent W.P.C. on the switchboard remembered the name of his current girlfriend and he was found at her flat. He was not pleased.

Mary had asked to come along but Jim Polk and her husband told her it was impossible. She had looked a little pale as she saw them off. In the taxi Polk remembered something.

"There's one thing you didn't explain," he said. "What about that note that was sent to the Principal; you thought it was the Registrar woman who wrote it."

"It might have been a red herring and I wasted a lot of thought over it. It was, of course written by Miss Penfold and she simply wanted to warn Floodgate ... to whom she is devoted ... of a possible scandal."

"But how did she know?"

"Jim, it's a great mistake in this detection business to think you're the only one who can work out a problem. She knew most of the facts and she's a highly intelligent woman, though a rather bad-tempered one. Perhaps, too, she had some information we haven't discovered. I think she knew."

In the taxi Polk had one more question.

"Why did Fordham go off and not the woman?"

"I told you: the whole operation was coming to an end and there was work to be done at Birmingham. I think, too, that someone at the College may have suspected that he was up to something ... we know who, don't we ... and he may have panicked a bit. The news of the murder must have been a terrible shock to him: I don't suppose he ever knew that the woman had a gun. Don't forget these are not professional criminals with cool nerves: just very greedy people; intelligent but inexperienced. For example, it was stupid to do the welding at the College: there was a perfectly good garage at the Larkhill house. They also left two very obvious clues there: the books on Africa and the bottle of Schnapps. They should also have known that a Radio transmitter can cause interference. Doesn't the Post Office have vans that go around checking. Definitely not Napoleons of Crime!"

"Napoleon! What's he got to do with it?"

"When you start reading detective stories, Jim, start with Sherlock Holmes."

* * * * *

Superintendent Garrett grudgingly agreed to Richard accompanying the party in the two Police Cars, the first containing himself, Morris and two Constables whose military style jackets bulged with protective padding. Polk, Bosworth, Richard and a uniformed officer were in the second car.

Polk had persuaded his superiors that a .45 revolver might be in the hands of a criminal prepared to use it and the two men in protective armour carried weapons. They drove to the Larkhill estate.

There was a thin rain failing and it was cold. The house was dark and the nearest street lamp was forty yards further up the road, the drivers pulling up some distance from the pool of light it provided. At a sign from Garrett one of the jacketed men and the uniformed Constable disappeared in the direction of the access lane that ran behind the houses. Number twenty was unlit and silent.

The Superintendent seemed undecided. He stood at the garden gate for a moment and whispered a few words to Morris. That officer in turn spoke to Richard.

"You're to keep right back, Sir, not being official. There could be a little trouble here."

Remembering Polk's description of the body of Henry Seaforth, shot down in cold blood at short range, Richard privately agreed and felt no urge to heroic action. Garrett rang the bell.

The chimes from within the house sounded eerie. There was no response and the officer rang twice more.

"Have to break it in," he said nervously. "Where's those tools, Bosworth?"

Bosworth advanced with a small bag that clinked as he set it down before the door. He took a small torch from his packet and selected what looked like a short crow-bar. From the garden gate Richard watched the scene. Before Bosworth could begin to work the door opened.

There was no light inside the house and the dark-clad figure who stood in the entrance could only be faintly made out. Superintendent Garrett spoke first.

"Trudi Pienaar ... I ..."

"Get back, all of you, or you are dead."

The voice had the flat vowels of South African speech but it also had a hard edge to it.

"Now, Miss ..."

"Get back: I do not joke."

From the rear of the house came a faint tinkling noise of a glass panel breaking. The woman heard it too and a hysterical note came into her voice.

"Do you think I shall give up now? Get back ... not to your car ... the other way ... quick!"

From behind her came the voice of one of the two men sent to the rear.

"Put it down, Miss ... it's no good resisting."

Trudi Pienaar spun round and Polk jumped forward. The gun roared: Richard had not realised that revolvers made such a loud noise and for a moment there was a confusion of bodies grappling in the doorway. Polk was clutching his left arm grazed by a bullet and the others were having surprising difficulty in handcuffing the struggling woman who was cursing them loudly in what Richard supposed was Afrikaans. It seemed to be a language well suited to the purpose and it is doubtful whether she heard Garrett's formal caution.

Bosworth and the two Constables got her into one of the two cars, and Morris, using the vehicles first aid kit bandaged Jim Polk's arm, rather unkindly pointing out that he was likely to give a stiff-armed performance in the coming pantomime. Superintendent Garrett delivered a stern rebuke to his junior officers.

"A real poor show on all counts. You should have known that I could have talked her round in an hour or so ... proper procedure. That young fool Elphinstone was only told to watch the rear entrance, not to barge in like that. And don't think, Jim Polk, that you'll get a commendation out of it ... talk about pantomimes, indeed! Have you thought how much paper work I'd have had if she'd aimed straight."

Richard, embarrassed, kept in the background.

* * * * *

The Chief Constable, brought from a ceremony at the Masonic Hall was very gracious. Sir Gregory Ogmore had not risen in the Force by merit but he had considerable charm.

"They tell me, Sir Richard, that you've given us some help again.

"Inspector Polk is very grateful, I'm sure. You and Lady Smith must come to dinner one evening and tell us how you set about these little problems."

"We should love to, Sir Gregory. May I say that I hope you will be able to keep my name out of this business. I don't suppose that I will be needed to give evidence in any legal proceedings."

"Of course, my dear boy: I quite understand. Shall we just say `on information received'. I will issue strict orders that your name is not to be mentioned."

Sir Ogmore might have saved his breath. The elderly Constable ... with no hope of promotion ... who had good contacts with several newspaper reporters was already on his way to a public telephone. Young Elphinstone was his nephew which meant that the generous fee that he expected would have to be shared. Almost before the Chief Constable had finished uttering platitudes, the Night Editor of the Daily Meteor was ordering the front-page headline to be changed.

Sir Gregory very kindly ordered a police car to take Richard home. The driver had heard something of the night's events and wanted to talk about it: his passenger was not to be drawn.

Mary heard the car pull up and opened their front door. She ran out and threw herself into his arms.

"You're all right? I was so worried: did she have a gun?"

"She did; and poor Jim got winged: only a scratch, though. I kept in the background. They'll charge her with Seaforth's murder and probably other things as well. You should have heard her swearing in Dutch!"

"What about Edward Fordham?"

"They'll find him. The Police will have it that he's gone abroad but I have a hunch that he isn't far away."

"Why do you think that?"

"Cringle: those two offers for the house that were quickly rejected. The estate agent must have known how to get in touch with him easily ... difficult if he was in Darkest Africa."

"I'm sure you're right. Would you like a Horlicks?"

* * * * *

The Daily Meteors scoop did not mean that the Smiths were spared harassment by press-men the next day. In the end Richard could only get rid of them by making a guarded statement to the man from a more or less respectable paper and even he reported most of what he was told in a garbled form. One or two were still hanging around the gates of India House when Polk arrived in the evening.

His arm was in a sling and he was driven by Sergeant Bosworth. The remaining reporters pounced on him, but the Inspector having received a stern rebuke the previous evening was not in the mood to make indiscretions and he soon got rid of them. Bosworth, invited to join the party would not stay ... he wanted to get back to his girlfriend from whose embraces he had ben so rudely torn the night before ... Polk settled in his usual chair.

"Well, that's all nicely cleared up. As I think I said, he hadn't gone abroad. Birmingham C.I.D. picked him up at his brother's place this morning. God knows what we can charge him with. He's not saying anything: he knows the ropes ... used to be a Barrister. You were wrong about one thing, Richard; he's not married to the Pienaar woman ... just the usual relationship: he had a wife who divorced him."

"Oh, well; married or not married, does it make much difference these days?"

"Yes it does," Mary put in, "and don't you start thinking differently, Richard Smith." As Polk left Richard reminded him.

"You lost your bet, Jim. Don't forget those tickets for the pantomime."

"They were delivered next day; but the show was dire!

* * * * *

They had their few days in Bristol and got back on Christmas Eve.

Richard had thought that Mary would look nice in a fur coat and had offered to buy her one during their visit. She declared that she had a moral objection to such garments and her husband's argument that if it was alright to wear leather shoes, furs should be permissible; cut no ice.

They enjoyed a quiet Christmas with Mary rather more pensive than usual. She even got Richard to church on Christmas morning to hear Canon Bassett's sermon on 'The Message of Bethlehem for the Environment'.

It was on Boxing Day morning that she gave him the news.

"I'm fairly certain this time: isn't it wonderful!"

Richard was no mathematician but as a detective he had calculated correctly and interpreted certain signs. He was, however, able to demonstrate pleasure and simulate surprise.

Wilde was not his favourite author but he remembered that Oscar had said:

"Only savages are sincere."